Sons of Darkness

TALES OF MEN, BLOOD AND IMMORTALITY

Edited by
Michael Rowe
and Thomas S. Roche

Published in the United States by Cleis Press Inc., P.O. Box 8933, Pittsburgh, Pennsylvania 15221, and P.O. Box 14684, San Francisco, California 94114.
Printed in the United States.
Cover and text design:
Logo art: Juana Alicia
First Edition.
10 9 8 7 6 5 4 3 2 1

"His Mouth Will Taste of Wormwood" by Poppy Z. Brite first appeared in *Borderlands,* edited by Thomas Monteleone. Avon Books, 1990. Copyright © 1990 by Poppy Z. Brite. Used by permission of the author.

Library of Congress Cataloging-in-Publication Data

Sons of darkness : tales of men, blood and immortality / edited
    by Michael Rowe and Thomas S. Roche. — 1st ed.
        p.   cm.
    ISBN 1-57344-059-0 (paper)
        1. Vampires—Fiction.   2. Gay men's writings, American.
3. Horror tales, American.   4. Gay men—Fiction.   I. Rowe,
Michael, 1962- . II. Roche, Thomas S.
    PS648.V35S65   1996
    813'.08738089206642—dc20   96-30717
                                                          CIP

Acknowledgments

In the spirit of friendship and respect between gay men and lesbians, Michael Rowe and Thomas S. Roche would like to thank Felice Newman and Frédérique Delacoste of Cleis Press—primarily a women's press—for their support of a book of gay male vampire stories. Our thanks are also due to Pam Keesey, who laid the groundwork with *Daughters of Darkness*, for her extraordinary sensitivity and insight into the queer vampire genre. Most importantly, we thank our authors—who represent a full spectrum of sexual orientations—for laying aside their differences and concentrating on a common vision that we hope will terrify and delight you.

Michael Rowe would like to acknowledge the longtime support of Evelyn Bezant of Smithbooks in Milton, Ontario, for her unfailing enthusiasm and many extraordinary kindnesses. Every writer should have the privilege of experiencing this level of commitment and friendship from someone in the trade. He is indebted to Tony Timpone and Michael Gingold for their friendship and their enthusiasm for his work at *Fangoria*, and to Don Hutchison, friend and mentor par excellence. Special thanks also to Michael Thomas Ford, Michael Lowenthal, and Ron Oliver, for the sort of friendship, understanding, and support that only another gay male writer can truly provide. And to Scott Dagostino and Janet Ferguson, who have always known exactly why.

Thomas S. Roche would like to acknowledge the assistance and inspiration of Lawrence Schimel, and the invaluable help and recommendations of Michael Thomas Ford, in helping flesh out this book. Pam Keesey deserves a special thank-you for her support, encouragement, and enthusiasm. Thanks also to whatever dark gods gave me the longtime support and friendship of Alex S. Johnson. Finally, thanks go to Hammer Studios and Chelsea Quinn Yarbro, for making me stay up all night—more than a few times.

Contents

For Tasia Hazisavvas and Werner Warga
—*Michael Rowe*

For David J. Howell
—*Thomas S. Roche*

Introduction

The taste of blood has grown foul in recent years. The Sons of Darkness cower in the night pronouncing unholy prayers, begging for release from the fate that has cursed them. The hunter has become the hunted, tracked by a merciless predator with an inhuman face and a name so cold and omnipresent, it's not even ominous anymore. The children of the night haunt their own tombs, afraid to taste ecstasy. They weep crimson tears and mutter halfhearted post-Stonewall requiems under their breath. They hide amid gravestones and crabgrass; they scrawl obscene sayings on the walls of their own sepulchers, hoping someone will see and be afraid.

Perhaps the vampire remembers a time when it was different: when he could hunt, drunk with power, knowing that his immortality was assured by that very lust for blood that drove him, knowing that the ecstasy of that forbidden draught would keep his heart beating long after the priests and their faithful had consigned his soul to God. Those glorious nights may seem over. But for those who crave blood, and whose craving sustains them through a thousand midnights, these nights of passion can never be over. As long as the moon shines, the blood lust will rise again. Such unholy things do not die—though they are, of course, beyond living.

The book you are holding in your hands is a result of a fortuitous collision between two writers, both of them longtime devotees of the vampire genre, Michael Rowe and Thomas S. Roche. While each of us was familiar with the other's work, and we had communicated about other publishing projects, we had never thought to talk about vampires. This might not seem strange to the average person. But the children of darkness are not average people. Never have been, never will be. The cool dark spell of the undead weaves itself

9

around a chosen few, and leaves the rest of the populace gaping, wondering what would compel an otherwise well-adjusted person to obsess about vampires, blood and immortality. It's no good trying to explain it—you're either bitten, or you're not. "Vampire people" find each other: Blood calls to blood.

When the two of us finally met in person at the San Francisco Bay Area Book Fair in November 1995 (close enough to Halloween that its echoes still played about the city), a mutual interest in vampires was discovered, and the idea for *Sons of Darkness* was born. Apart from vampires and the role they had played in both our cultural and erotic inner landscapes, the two of us had very little else in common; we represented two fragments of the very eclectic community of vampire devotees. We had grown up on opposite sides of the continent—Roche in the United States, Rowe in Canada—yet somehow we had both been caught in the same spell. The same books and films had cast a dark shadow across our disparate lives.

There were elements to our lives that seemed programmed to make us brothers of the night. As queer writers whose work had often dealt with alternative and radical sexuality, we had both developed some sense of alienation from what we felt was the mainstream of society. We had always known what it meant—both metaphorically and literally—to walk the dark streets in the moonlight, finally knowing both the freedom and terror of the night, while our more respectable colleagues slept.

The vampire *is* queer, by definition. It is no accident that the public's fascination with vampires has always occurred at times of shifting sexuality and growing conservatism: In repressive Victorian England was born Count Dracula; the paranoid and depressed 1930s, following the decadent and sensualist twenties, were haunted by the vampire films of Universal Pictures, and by Bela Lugosi, who will forever serve as film's defining vampire. The conservative and (in the United States) McCarthy-badgered late 1950s brought Hammer Studio's *Horror of Dracula*, and its many sequels rode the wave of newfound sexual permissiveness, the women's movement, lesbian and gay rights, the countercultural youth movements, and everything else that the 1960s had to offer. Now, of course, in the age of AIDS and the sex-phobia it has engendered, come a revival of gothic culture and a widespread interest in vampires.

Vampires terrify in order to delight. They give voice and form to dark sexuality and bring well-deserved death to mundanity. They let us fly on the icy wind of the night, and live forever in the shadows, away from the rules of society. Vampires cause us to question at what price pleasure, and at what price immortality. They show us that choices are dangerous—and lack of choices even more dangerous. To appropriate an expression from another radical social movement, close to at least one editor's heart: vampires fuck shit up.

The literary establishment against which we are laying out *Sons of Darkness* is a highly sophisticated one—nourished, not inconsequentially, by Pam Keesey's lesbian vampire anthologies, *Daughters of Darkness* and *Dark Angels*, both published by Cleis Press. In 1991, Alyson Publications produced a spate of gay "horror" literature, including *Embracing the Dark*, edited by Eric Garber; a novel, *Vampires Anonymous*, and a Lambda Literary Award-winning collection of short stories, *Somewhere in the Night*, both by Jeffrey N. McMahon.

Our reasons for choosing *Tales of Men, Blood and Immortality* as a subtitle, rather than *Gay Vampire Stories*, were manifold. Just as the two of us represent some of the contradictions in queer culture today (Michael identifies as "gay," while Thomas uses the label "queer"), *Sons of Darkness* also reflects certain contradictions and ambiguities. Sex radicals (including those two problematic creatures of the night, the bisexual and the transsexual) have muddied the waters of gender and sexuality in recent years; who is to say what constitutes "gay" anymore, let alone "gay fiction," let alone a "gay vampire," let alone a "gay vampire story"? Furthermore, the eroticism of the vampire goes so deeply beyond conventional mortal hungers that, when it bites the reader, it shatters existing notions of everything—which is the whole point. *Sons of Darkness* collects stories about men in contact with other men, in the badlands where all that matters is terror and hunger and need—and that terror, that hunger, that need, more completely describe the essence of homoeroticism than any label.

By the same token, as two queer writers working in the horror genre, we have long noticed that it often does not matter to a story what the sexual orientation of the vampire is: Being a vampire, like being an S/M devotee, ought to transcend sexual orientation. You are a vampire, or you are a vampire's victim. The vampire's power to lure is rooted in his power to seduce. Many are the men who have watched Christopher Lee towering at the head of that stone stairwell, eyes burning, teeth bared, and thought: *Someone get rid of that whimpering bodice-ripped heroine and let me take her place.* Christopher Lee's Dracula is the ultimate top. A life of nights seems a small price to pay for such erotic power.

This has certainly been the case with Anne Rice's vampire novels, which have such a rich queer following. Rice herself has said that her vampires transcend sexual orientation, and in spite of the outcry over Tom Cruise's portrayal of Lestat in the film version of *Interview with the Vampire* not being homoerotic enough, the fact is that Lestat and Louis's relationship in the film is undeniably spousal, and intricately interwoven. They are forever young and forever handsome predators, but to call either of them "gay" seems out of place. Calling them "queer" is even sillier. They are men, they are vampires, and they are immortal.

Similarly, in the stories in *Sons of Darkness,* "orientation" has often been made secondary to desire. C. Dean Andersson's "My Greatest Fear" touches on deep themes of betrayal and redemption. Kevin Killian's "Click" alludes to a modern kind of vampiric relationship that appears at first glance a bit less sanguine than traditional vampirism. Carol Queen delves into the metaphors of sexuality and sustenance in "Feeding." William J. Mann's "Waiting for the Vampire" brings the terror of anticipation to a crescendo, and D. Travers Scott's "Tongues" takes the undead into cyberspace, another sort of shadowland. David Nickle's "Sick Reggie" gives us a dark tale of illness and predation. In "Retribution for Golgotha," Wickie Stamps brings us her trademark lush grotesquerie that fascinates as well as repulses. "Wet" by M. Christian brings themes of liquidity and art to the forefront, and Nancy Kilpatrick gives us a deceptively seductive and ultimately vicious take on the games men play. Ron Oliver's "Bela Lugosi is Dead" casts a well-deserved shadow over Beverly Hills. Poppy Z. Brite's classic "His Mouth Will Taste of Wormwood" is one of the most lushly erotic vampire stories ever written. And Pat Califia, who is responsible for plenty of darkness herself, lulls us with a brutal and beautiful tale of a vampire at a cruel turning point of gay history.

These stories terrify in order to delight; they cast shadows in order to illuminate. They will suck the blood from your veins and the marrow from your bones. You will taste flesh and blood, and the night will look that much more beautiful.

Pleasant nightmares.

Introduction

In the heart of the vampire, only one thing can defeat its hunters. The lust for flesh and blood alone can bring the children of the night out of their hiding places, alive but unliving, slain but undead, murderous in the extreme and hungry for the taste of living flesh. And then the hunters of the vampire shall be brought to their knees. The wrath of the vampire is a terrible thing. And having sown the wind, the hunters shall reap the whirlwind.

The lust for flesh and blood is eternal. The crypts of its devotees may be cracked open and set aflame. Its believers may be murdered and hunted and persecuted. But tonight when the sun scatters molten blood across the horizon, and the gentle serenade of the crickets whispers its subtle invitation—

Then, the need for blood shall reign supreme. The Sons of Darkness shall again rule their master's kingdom.

And among the mortals, even kings and killers shall weep in terror.

Michael Rowe and Thomas S. Roche
San Francisco, November 1995 —
Toronto, July 1996 —

My Greatest Fear

C. DEAN ANDERSSON

for David... "Who's winning?"
Go ahead and grin.

He stretched naked on the cold slab and looked at me with glowing eyes from beneath long-lashed, half-closed lids. His lips formed a Mona Lisa smile.

"You're the best, Puppy Boy." He yawned. "I'm getting sleepy. I guess that means He'll be here, soon."

By the flickering light of the candle I'd brought with me, I checked my watch. "Yeah, soon." My warm breath made puffs of steam in the frigid air. "Almost dawn."

I pulled on my pants, socks, boots and sweatshirt. I found my parka and slipped it on, too, then I took a cigarette from a crumpled pack in my coat pocket and lit up.

He patted the slab.

I sat down but didn't look at him.

He gently touched the side of my face with his cold fingers. "Look at me, Puppy Boy."

I did not look at him.

He pulled back his hand. "Is something wrong?"

I barked a laugh. "That's kind of an understatement, don't you think?"

"Didn't you like me...like this? Or are you still angry with me?"

I sucked on my cigarette.

"You can't still be angry with me, not after all you've seen."

I looked him in the face. "Nothing I've seen or heard changes the fact that you left me and our home, for Him and for *this!*" I made a throwaway gesture at his ugly little tomb.

"In case you weren't listening earlier, I did this, *became this,* for us."

"Yeah, right."

"You've *got* to understand!"

"I don't have to do anything. You're the one who has to do things, now, like drinking blood and being a corpse while the sun is up."

"Oh, get me my hip boots, darlin', 'cause the shit's gettin' deep as hell in here."

"Well, you should know about Hell."

"Grow up and get over it. Your religion is kaput! Gone with the wind. There's no God, no Devil, no Heaven, no Hell. There's just good ole Life and bad ole Death and pretty-much-okay-most-of-the-time Undeath."

"According to you."

"I didn't make this reality. I just discovered it. And you say I'm the one who has to do things, now? Like you *don't* have to do anything? What about dying? That's what you *are* doing, remember? Just like I was before I found the Blood Boys and learned how to make a deal with the Reaper. Cross my heart and hope not to die, it's the *only* way to beat Him! And all you have to do to beat Him, too, is to join me in Undeath."

"This thing you've become…it's *worse* than Death."

"Bullshit!"

I ground out my cigarette on the side of his stone slab. "You don't know what it was like, sitting here yesterday afternoon, waiting for sunset. I would say your name, touch you, kiss you, but you didn't respond to anything I did. When *He* came, though, when *He* kissed you, *then* you responded, came back to life, moaned in ecstasy like you were really getting off on Him, and—"

"You're jealous!" His cold fingers touched my face again, slipped downward and stroked my throat.

I pushed his hand away.

He laughed. "It's silliness on a scale of infinity to be jealous of the Reaper. You might as well be jealous of the Sun or Moon. I love your kisses. You *know* that. But His Kiss? It's not just physical. It's spiritual ecstasy, like touching stars, riding on comets, drinking moonlight. It sounds like hippy-dippy corn, but it really is like being one with the Cosmos! And the Undead experience the Kiss each dawn and each sunset. It's the spirituality Trip-o-lay Supreme. It's Mondo Ecstasy for the soul with a cherry on top. It's—"

"Cut the crap."

"But crap it's not. It's the pure dee-lux-orama and completely naked truth. And it's how we can survive, *together!* You can make a deal with Him, just like I did. But you don't have to go through those creepola Blood Boys. You can let *me* be the one who initiates you with a Bloodkiss. It's so easy—"

"And what about *our* deal?"

"Dear One, this beats the hell out of a double suicide. Only an idiot would prefer being dead with me to being Undead with me."

"Well, maybe I *am* an idiot. I never claimed to be as smart as you. I couldn't get a job as fancy as the one you had."

"Please, not another blue collar self-pity party."

"But I've always worked hard at the jobs I could get, and I've always been faithful and true to you."

"Sounds like a high school pep song."

"Right. Okay. I wanted to try and explain something to you, but what's the use? You'd never understand. You—"

"Shhh!"

I heard it. He was returning.

The sound was like someone walking in dead leaves, a rustling, crackling, dry and dusty sound. Then the shadows in one corner condensed into a tall, dark shape, the classic image of Death, a skeleton draped in a hooded black cloak.

I imagined the Reaper being simultaneously anywhere and everywhere that one of the Undead walked or slept whenever sunset or sunrise touched the Earth, a Being not constrained by the physical laws of space and time. I felt a deep chill. I stepped away from the slab.

The Reaper looked at me. No light glowed in His empty eye sockets. His skeletal grin mocked me. I felt an urge, deep and primal, to go to Him, but I resisted.

I shook my head, no. Not yet. Not until I'd done what I had left to do.

He flitted like a shadow soundlessly to the slab, bent down with a jerk, and touched His fleshless teeth to my lover's lips.

The Kiss of Sleep had been bestowed.

My lover sighed in ecstasy, then grew silent, stopped breathing.

The Reaper vanished.

A corpse now lay naked on the slab. We couldn't talk again until the Reaper kissed him awake at sunset. But there wasn't anything left to talk about, anyway. So, I went home. But I did not go to sleep.

I gathered what I needed and returned to the tomb.

Only one thing now could make things right. Having seen my loved one as he had become and having made love to his repulsively cold flesh had only strengthened my resolve.

But I was horribly afraid.

I was not afraid that I would fail to do what needed to be done, nor that I would fail to send myself to the Reaper afterward. No.

I'd read the stories, seen the movies. Images of Vampires' eyes snapping open and of screaming, pain-distended mouths filled my mind. And that was my greatest fear.

I didn't want my lover to see and hate me in his last moments. I didn't want the stake to make him scream.

Click

KEVIN KILLIAN

His offhand ways had given George Dorset access to the city's most beautiful bodies—for his photographic studies—yet these were the ones that most quickly cloyed on him. If they were available, George confided, then their blood was "wrong." Too sweet. "It's like, they're giving everything up, and I don't like that," he told me, flashing his sharp grin. "You're looking at a guy who gets discouraged, like, real quick. I don't go for the easy ones.

"I had a masterpiece one time," he advised. We were sitting side by side at the Castro Theater waiting for the lights to go down. Onstage an organist was playing a medley of tunes from *West Side Story* in that insinuating squeaky drone that always tweaks one's nerves. I could smell George's scent, underneath his casual eighties' Girboud jacket. While he reminisced I drank in his smell like fizzy water. "Want to hear about my masterpiece?" He nudged me, spilling popcorn, and I nodded, my eyes fixed on his face.

"Sure," I said, "whatever, George."

He let out a sigh in the hot quiet air of the packed theater. "His name was Tommy," he said. "Tommy Calhoun. Beautiful meat. But there was a setback, my friend. Turned out he didn't want me. That was my great setback, my masterpiece was straight."

George was the first vampire I ever knew. At least he *said* he was one—I never was sure. There's bullshit everywhere, especially in graduate school where he and I met. Maybe he was, maybe he wasn't—I have an open mind, I'm a liberal.

At first I thought there was some heat between us, but I was wrong. Wasn't my fault, he said. I was just too brainy. He liked the dumb ones. George Dorset was a picky son of a bitch, why didn't he want my blood? Dear reader, I really wanted to fuck him but I just couldn't get in his pants. Because of my blood. My blood and brains and the way the latter put a chemical spin on the former, this total bullshit. "Too sour," he said, with a moue. "It's almost as if the higher the IQ, the blood spoils really really fast. I'm a grown guy and I've been around for centuries. I want it perfect every time. Has to be a straight dumb stud like in a porn tape."

"You're spoiled," I said. All photographers are, and George had this added vampire thing to really give him this smug "been-there done-that" expression.

"Ah, actually I'm not," he chided. "I might have been, true, but don't forget, I lost the one guy who I really loved, and everyone else since then has just been this kind of replacement for him, for my Irish beauty Tommy Calhoun."

Okay, I was kind of miffed. I'm Irish too, I thought. I felt like Barbra Streisand in *On a Clear Day You Can See Forever:* confronted with the aristocratic Melinda, refined in Regency Cecil Beaton empire dresses and feathers and marquise wigs, New York hippie squawker Daisy Gamble just about—dies of shame. She tumbles around her psychiatrist's office, swinging from poles, belting out her big torch number—"What Did I Have (That I Don't Have?)" But George Dorset, it turned out, had never seen this classic 1970 Vincente Minnelli color spectacular. I was, like, frankly, shocked. Just then the lights went down in the movie house and I reached for George's hand and he closed his hand around mine, in the darkness. I could pretend I was his boyfriend, in the dark. The spooky credits came on for *Black Sunday,* with Barbara Steele and John Richardson. Villagers drive a mask of iron spikes into Barbara's face in, like, the first five seconds. George leaned to me and whispered, "It only gets better and better."

Not that Tommy Calhoun was any *aristocrat,* far from it. Tommy Calhoun who, when first spied by George, sat slumped on a bench in the park in a pair of faded dungarees, the cuffs rolled up, and a white sleeveless polo shirt. Some inner prompt had made George approach him, step by step, till he stood before the boy, close enough to breathe in his smell, *want some pictures to give your girl?* In that boyish serious face George saw recognition, the exquisite pain of consciousness stirring. So George took him to his studio uptown and posed Tommy against a snowy backdrop, telling him about his face's potential. "You take good pictures?" Tommy had asked.

"Who cares? You do," George replied. "Now how about you get

more comfortable, what are you wearing under those jeans?" "Not much," Tommy admitted, "but I'm keeping them on if it's all the same to you." Three weeks later, as agreed, he returned to pick up the pictures of his face, and some more spending money. "I like this arrangement," Tommy said. "You take good pictures," George said.

But there wasn't any fag stuff. George remembered asking Tommy, and Tommy's impassive refusal. His head, shaking no, his shrewd foxy face pursing its lips, *No, no, George.* A few drinks later Tommy's pants were down to his knees, then George pulled them off and threw them over the folding screen he kept in the studio for medical layouts. Stark naked Tommy stood, weaving, hands folded behind his back as directed, cock swinging no. "No fag stuff you said." "I'll make you feel so good," George said, moving in, touching the tip of Tommy's dick with one inquiring finger.

He laughed. "Forget it, okay!" And the picture George held in his hand now, of Tommy's face, was like a living reminder of his mocking stupid laugh. He waved a hand around the darkness that surrounded him, weaved his hand through it till it touched the extraordinary collection of light that gathered around Tommy Calhoun's face. "You straight?" he gasped.

"Yeah, man," said the boy.

"Tilt your neck like this," George whispered, and Tommy complied, baring the worked muscles in his neck, till the vein seemed to float up out of his skin. "That's it," George said. He wondered what Tommy heard, in his last moments, if he heard anything but a muffled series of syllables. "Thffff fffff." The vein that bulged from his neck like a ten penny nail set on the taut skin. All the locks in the studio snapping shut. Tommy stiffened as George bit into his throat, stiffened like a popsicle. Then the blood burst from his neck and he grew limper and limper till his heart stopped beating, no more blood left to move around like sludge. His eyes grew pale, his mouth slack. George held him in his arms like the *Pietà*, then dubbed his death a tragic accident, started to cry real tears.

Alone, George stands before the bath of chemicals in his apartment, takes a pair of tongs to lift a new print from the tray. Dripping with clear fluid, it wavers in the slight breeze. He doesn't understand, though he labors mightily to know, what makes a photograph different from real life. For one thing, you need the right angle: turn this photo over and all you'll see is a white square, whereas in Life when you look at something's backside you get the best view by far. He holds up another photo of Tommy Calhoun—alive—for my inspection.

"And since then," he told me, "I've been really beating the bushes to find his equal!" George's was the tragedy of all great artists: he saw things upside down. It was almost as though he wanted me to feel sorry for him! God, it would have been comical if I hadn't felt, you know…rejected kind of?

Like—my blood was *sour* like some old cheese at a party? Spank you very much as Jim Carrey says.

Possessed by the hunt, George drove into the wilderness for the nth time, in his big bumpy Ford. Camera slung round his neck, he rubbed its smooth bulb. Driving and rubbing gave him a hard-on. Which was fine. The roads were primitive, rocky; he thought of Walker Evans, jogging Appalachian roads to document the "pure products of America." This thinking, added to driving and rubbing, added a hard-on atop his hard-on—like an extra squeeze from a tube of Crest.

A strip of blue sky hung above the forest road and below his visor. George's eyes kept moving, eluding the sun.

It didn't take him long to find a pair who might submit adequately to him. Matched set: a father and son. Busily occupied with hoes and a wheelbarrow in their neat front yard. When the Ford pulled up their gravel driveway, the father pulled a handkerchief across his sweaty face, and this gesture alone told George he'd come to the right place. In a few curt sentences, he'd made father and son aware of the threat that hovered in the air. The A-Bomb. The H-Bomb. Hadn't the father and son heard about nuclear tests being conducted right over the Bay? "No, sir, we haven't."

"I did," said Paul, the fourteen year old. "In school I heard something like that."

"You did and kept hush about it?" asked his father.

"I *think* I did," Paul said.

"You two guys better come with me," said George, displaying his official papers, his badge, his stethoscope, his gun. "Loose lips sink ships," he warned them.

"Who are you anyway?" they asked. Then he told them who he was:

"FBI Doctor."

Mac replaced his hoe sturdily against the shed's side and hitched up his pants. Out of the side of his mouth he spat brown juice, then said, "Do what the man says, boy."

Paul stood irresolute halfway up the porch steps. George felt his tongue swell up in his mouth like a hot water bottle, felt the darkness descend from his visor like a cloud of flies. *That boy,* he thought, *is my tentative meat boy.*

"Shouldn't I tell Mom where we're going?"

Mac looked at George; George shook his head almost imperceptibly.

"Your mother don't have to know about this," Mac said. "Hustle here, Paulie. You heard: hustle."

Morosely, the three climbed into George's car. George could have said nothing, but he took pity on Paul, and as he backed carefully out the driveway, he said to the boy, "Always obey your father, son. He knows what's best. That's the American way."

"Yes, sir," Paul said, having made himself as small as possible in the big back seat, shrinking up against one wall. In the seat next to him, George was glad to see Paul's father praying silently, hands clenched, knuckles white. "Can I play with your FBI badge, sir?" said Paul to George Dorset. "I mean—like examine it over?"

Paul's was a face that flushed easily, like a postwar toilet, and George might have expected that the skin of Paul's butt would correspond to his face.... His father was more sanguine, less prone to quick changes in emotional barometer: the armed forces had done this to him; therefore his ass was both more and less interesting to watch than his son's. "Now hold still for the camera," George said.

Face down, Paul shook on the bed, his legs pressed tight together in the way of the shy child. Mac was less circumspect—again, the Service had inured him to submission—and showed an ease before George's camera and tripod that was almost as gratifying as Paul's embarrassment. It was the contrast, George decided, that provided the intrigue. The bedroom was cold and prim, decorated with lace and blackened etchings. In one corner stood a pile of old *Reader's Digests* from years back; Mac's toes, eager to please, touched it when George told him to. George studied the four legs before him, and raised and lowered a curtain, adjusted a meter. He couldn't "see" light, but he could watch it hover around others, give them color and sense. Paul's hair was red, his father's dusty brown, and along their legs the hairs willy-nilly combined in all shades. "It's medical," Mac said, to reassure his son. "It's nuclear."

"Legs farther apart," George said. "We're dealing with atom alpha here," he said sternly. "Paul, get those pants down along your ankles, c'mon, purple heart. Be brave. Look at your Dad."

"I don't like doctors," Paul whispered, his face a foot from his father's. George's camera began to whirl.

"You're gonna *be* a doctor, don't forget," Mac said, holding back his disgust at his son's cowardice. "What are you, chicken now? You're a big boy."

"I'm all right," Paul said.

"Good boy."

"Paul, you have two buttocks. Pull them apart."

"I wiped you," Mac said, pulling his own ass to strong pieces. "You don't remember, 'cause I went overseas so soon." The camera clicked and clacked like a Morse code key or a Geiger counter. The grimacing assholes of the father and son gleamed luridly in the shadowy room; in the aesthetic chamber of the camera's innards they became two rubies or licking flames. "You're a big boy now."

Paul held it. Convicted at last, he humped the camera. And after awhile, George drew in closer, towards the licking flames, those red rubies, that made his tongue and teeth feel so big in his mouth, that forced open his jaw…. Next thing he knew, his camera was clicking underneath his feet. He opened his eyes. He was lying on top of the two bodies, which were shredded up like ham salad. Blood spattered the walls of the cottage, even the *Reader's Digests* were damp, black slashes of drying blood curling the covers; he screamed. Click. Click.

George was at least five hundred years old, but to me he looked like a young person of about twenty-seven: a firm upper lip, red-tanned face, fierce eyes expressing disdain and interest both, short-cut black hair, and I remember his own ejaculate dripping from his brow, nose, chin. He took my picture, rubbed his fat dick up and down with one big hand while the other fiddled with knobs and meters on the camera's dark face. My lashes and pubic hair bristled under the harsh white light of the camera's scrutiny.

I met George in grad school one day when a woman was giving an "oral report" on Poe's *Narrative of A. Gordon Pym*. She talked about the possible sex symbolism in the name of Pym's alter ego. The name was Dirk Peters. Helplessly she threw up her hands and said, "Well, I say it's there if you want to play with it," or "play around with it." Can't remember now. But anyhow George's eyes met mine, and both of us began to laugh. No one else at the seminar table seemed to have caught Marilyn's little slip. And then afterwards, one thing led to another, and another had led to this photograph; but so few people have ever had one thing lead to another in their lives, that I couldn't help feeling an important dignity and beatitude in my informal, grotesque posing.

It *meant* something to me—but what? It had meant something to George, too. Possibly, I theorized, a hangover from childhood, when "Say Cheese," "Watch the birdie," and "Click! Took your picture!" had conveyed, to a child at least, a set of invitations to some other world, some other kind of…bird world. No wonder then that George had seduced so many, who had not thought they wanted seduction, by the simple prospect of asking them to strip to nothing. Americans, he said, *want* "nothing," they'll fuck their mothers to get there.

Did I want to see what made George tick? he asked. Well, I did and I didn't. You can tell I was ambivalent. I went to his apartment, nervous, the walls gloomy and oppressive, on a cool October morning, just before lunchtime.

George stood before the refrigerator in a short-sleeved shirt and a pair of chinos. The door was open, and an array of bottled salad dressings lined a metal rack inside, under the protective shadow of a platter of cold meats, heaped high and greasy. "Sandwich?" he asked. I shook my head. A bottle of beer apiece. We passed through the cold rooms where George lived: the magazines folded open to pages of good-looking men; the pictures, unframed, leaning up against the crinkled yellow wallpaper; the dim wattage overhead. An oversized poster of Barbara Steele, looking mysterious, her white face wreathed in a black streaming fog, huge dark eyes ablaze with hatred. *An Angel for Satan*, it said, in lurid red letters, below her name and face. George carried a tray laden with Wonder bread and Hellmann's mayonnaise, and showed me into a room with a tall ceiling. "When you want something quick, in a hurry," he said, "nothing's better than a sandwich and a bottle of beer." "Thanks for the

tip. 'For a more gracious lifestyle…' " "Like my room, smart ass?"
One wall was lined with books, a desk fronted another wall, and
there was a cabinet with his books of photos, protected from the
sun's feeble rays by a towel. In faded blue across the towel's thin
white cotton I read the name *Hotel Collingwood.* I turned on my
heel and idled myself in front of the east window.

George whisked the towel away like a magician parting a curtain,
and flashed me his hard white smile. "Ready to roll?"

We sat, dodging broken springs on a low chintz-covered couch,
and he showed me his photo albums, one after another like job
applicants. "They're all here—the bad and the beautiful." His years
of documentation. I felt light-headed, dizzy, dizzy enough to pick
up one of the bologna sandwiches. *Okay, I thought, okay. Let's find
out what makes him tick.*

George opened a thick black book with the portentous air of an
undertaker showing you your seat at a wake. "Are these your victims?" I said. I brushed crumbs from my lap, which George had
turned into a sex show. "They are victims," he intoned, "of their
own great vanity." He pointed to one picture, in which a man and
boy knelt at the foot of a bed bent over, showing their assholes to
the camera. Their hands grabbing the flesh of their hips to uncover
the asshole. George said, gently, "Father and son."

"How did you get them to do that?"

He explained his ruse: FBI doctor. Showed me his badge and his
wallet, larded with cooked-up IDs under a dozen different names,
told me about the Mission liquor store you could buy them at.

"I like the context," George said, scanning the print closely. "I've
always had a weakness for—generations, you might say. If you did-
n't know they were father and son, what would you think? You ever
wonder what your own father looks like, naked? I did," he said.
"When he was dying I got my big chance, pulled down the bedcov-
ers, old man lying there out like a light, the cancer smell coming off
him strong enough to knock you down."

And he'd seen: just this tube with skin grown over it, mashed up,
dead white skin. And he'd seen: withered balls, withered fruit, in a
nest of skin like the white leaves of nasturtium. Magpie's nest, but
strangely identifiable as the source of his own being, this ugly maze
of rolled meat and age…. He wanted to get up and run, before his

father woke, before the death of his father. "There's a story in the Bible, in Genesis," he told me, "the drunkenness of Noah?"

"I don't know it."

"I forget, you're ignorant. Noah, right? The one with the Ark?"

"Yes, George," I said, clenching my teeth. "I've heard of Noah."

"When Noah was an old man, he had three sons—Ham, Japheth and Shem. One day he got drunk and his clothes fell off him, in the presence of his three sons. Evidently this was a big taboo, seeing the nakedness of your father. Ham, the bad son, laughed. The two good sons covered up dear old Dad with a blanket till he slept it off."

"But why do you do this?" I cried out. "All these photos!"

He continued as though I had said nothing. "So for his sin of laughter, Ham was banished from Israel. Some say he went to Africa. In the eighteenth and nineteenth centuries, this text was used as a justification of slavery, since blacks were thought of as the sons and daughters of Ham, the inferior brother. But actually I think Ham might have been the first vampire."

Exasperated I flicked through the pages of the album on my lap, as fast as the wings of a butterfly flying. The bodies on the pages seemed to be twisting and turning in some infernal fire, their smiles and blank looks melting into a final demonic grimace. Maybe that's too strong. Actually they looked as if they were having sex, and most of them were.

"Are some of these guys hundreds of years old?" I asked. "Are these studs from the seventeenth century or whatever?"

He threw me a look of scorn. "Photography's a recent invention," he said. "All things put together. Before, say, 1850, you couldn't photograph someone if you wanted to. You couldn't keep his image before you, as a treasure forever."

"How were people remembered then?"

God, tears nearly came to his eyes. "There *wasn't* much memory," he said. "I could express it in RAM, like a few K. Say you and I were living back then—and I left you," he began. "And you had no photograph of me. What would happen? Unless you hired some oil painter to paint me, you'd forget me real quick. My image would not float in front of your face. That's why," he said, patting my knee, "I had to keep coming back, to remind those I left of what I looked like. Life in the seventeenth century was like something out of an Oliver Sacks case history. Every time you opened your eyes you'd forgotten everything you ever knew."

"Oh," I said. "Wow. Painful."

"People tell me vampires don't come out in the daytime, but they don't know what it's like being me. It's as though a cloud of darkness surrounds me, clinging to my clothes, to my face. I see through darkness, all you shiny bright people who live and die. I see you all—white rabbits, absolutely outlined in whiteness upon a black background."

First George shut the book, then opened it again, wearing an expression that seemed to be saying, "I tried to tell him, but he was too dumb to understand." And oh, how I was straining to figure him out, so much my brain hurt! Even his knees looked attractive, his knees peeking out from the big glossy photo album he pulled into his lap, as though to protect himself from me. His knees, covered in denim, were like two blue knobs of speechless desire—I wanted to clutch them like a baby clutches his mother's breast.

He turned another page and pointed to another glossy square. "Here's my masterpiece…who I met much later—in 1952 in fact. Look," George said. A bed, a room. Moonlight lay like a white film on the bed, except in its far reaches where night hid in the thick darkness of black velvet. A clutter of tangled sheets, a boy's body twisted in sleep, head covered by a pillow, his finely muscled legs pointing in two directions, but limp, as though someone had injected him with morphine. Prominent and stark, ivory in the camera's eye, his butt stole all available light and glowered there. Beyond, the other fittings of the room faded into a medley of dark and darker angles and smudges.

"That's Tommy Calhoun," he said, "who I met at the Y. The man who got away. You open a can of peaches, two of them bob up to the top. That was his backside: perfect," George said, almost as if he were alone. "Perfect ass." With both hands I took George's wrist and shook it away from my crotch.

"Hey, come on, Kevin. I *know* I stirred you up a bit, south of the border. I thought maybe a little handjob," George said.

"You thought wrong," I replied. My heart like a lump of cold steel in my chest.

"His name was Tommy," said George, watching the photo, as if it might jump from his sight. "He had the blood of a great knight, slithering through this wonderful boy's body. I could have eaten his blood for the rest of my life, but I let him get away, his death over-ruled me."

Well, there was something kind of sad about his tale, but I was fighting off my own feelings—which were a complicated fusion of lust, annoyance and fear. I wanted him, but he didn't want me—not really. I kept thinking if he's a vampire, he's scared of garlic, crosses, rivers, all this stuff I learned from watching Hammer movies and taking courses in Bram Stoker. Vampires, I recalled, don't show up in photos—I frowned, trying to remember where I'd put my own Brownie camera. Thinking I'll smuggle it in here and snap a picture of George, see what develops. Then thinking: well, maybe that wouldn't be cool; maybe, actually, I didn't want to know.

"Wish my dad could see me now," George told me. "There's a cer-tain kind of guy I'm real attracted to; I want a dumb guy, a hick. Just like my dad. I'm always looking for this type guy. I mean, there's a certain number of places you find the dumbos, so that's where I go. Bars. Pool halls. Gyms. And then, one day, I found him."

He told me about following his masterpiece boy from his apart-ment to the Y, where they'd struck up an acquaintance.

Tommy's pants were shoved to his knees, and George whispered to him from across the room, *Feel it, feel it, and think of your girl.* And slowly Tommy put his hand around his cock and concentrated on her. This absent woman. And slowly it rose up in his hand and became the great symbol of absence for George; it became for George a living, wily thing that had the rest of him by the balls. And George hid behind his camera and took his picture.

Glazed over, Tommy's eyes became twin wax seals George could-n't get through or penetrate. His wide, full "go-to-Hell" mouth. I still keep the picture: as I write this it lies on my desk under the cool white beam of a tensor lamp. I wish I could show it to you proper-ly, but even if I were able to reproduce it perfectly, it could not give the flowerlike beauty of Tommy's coloring, the red-gold hair, the sea-blue eyes, the exquisite flush of exultant youth that played about him like an enchantment; but perhaps even its cold, black-and-white shadow of a laughing boy in a torn T-shirt would give you enough of a suggestion of his warm enchantment to make the incredible disaster that resulted from that enchantment more credi-ble. "But you know what I think about the sons of Ham," George said wistfully. "Ham wasn't the first African—*I* don't think. I think he was the first vampire." At home in my little apartment, filled with pictures and books, I opened the Bible to find out more about George, more about Tommy. "And Noah began to *be* a husband-man," I read, "and he planted a vineyard:

"And he drank of the wine, and was drunken; and he was uncovered within his tent." Click.

"And Ham, the father of Canaan, saw the nakedness of his father, and told his two brothers without." Click.

"And Shem and Japheth took a garment, and laid *it* upon both their shoulders, and went backward, and covered the nakedness of their father; and their faces *were* backward, and they saw not their father's nakedness." Click.

"And Noah awoke from his wine, and knew what his younger son had done unto him." Click.

"And he said, Cursed *be* Canaan. A servant of servants shall he be unto his brethren." Click.

"And he said, Blessed *be* the Lord God of Shem; and Canaan shall be his servant." Click.

"God shall enlarge Japheth, and he shall dwell in the tents of Shem; and Canaan shall be his servant." Oh wow, I'm thinking. That tells me a lot! Next time I tried calling George, the operator said his number was disconnected or "out of service." I ran across town to his apartment, no sign of him anywhere. Even the walls had been painted over, not a scrap of him left. "Where did he go?" I asked the landlord, a burly man of Mongolian extraction. He shrugged, shot me a dour glance, went on replacing the lock. "And *was* he a vampire?" I asked zillions of my friends, who all got bored with *that* one real quick. Some friends! That was years ago. I remembered that George seemed oblivious to Barbra Streisand's power and beauty, yet, paradoxically, he loved Barbara Steele, the English actress who made so many horror films in Italy in the sixties—like *Black Sunday,* where she's the embodiment of evil in the more lively of her dual roles. I too became a devotee of Barbara Steele's oeuvre, and once, a few years ago at the Roxie Theater here in San Francisco, had the opportunity to meet Miss Steele in person, during a day-long appreciation of her work in cinema. "Can you pose for a picture with me, Miss Steele?" I begged. "Certainly," said she. As the camera clicked, I saw my opportunity. "Do you believe there are vampires?" I whispered to her. Her enormous dark eyes seemed to quiver—a gaze you could fall into, like the pitiless hole of Hell. She turned to me quickly. There was a rain of flashbulbs, white halogen light clouding our faces. I blinked. "Young man," she whispered, "I *know* there are."

Feeding

CAROL QUEEN

Sebastien stood on the lodge deck overhanging the river rushing and splashing far below. On certain nights the view from here filled him with melancholy—at dusk, as it was now, with shadows lengthening all around him, he longed sometimes to throw himself over the low stone rail, tumble down the steep sides of the rocky gorge. Would that, at last, end everything? No rash act he'd ever committed had managed to do more than momentarily stun him.

But this was only a few gloomy minutes stolen out of an otherwise busy evening. At length he would sigh and go back into the lodge—there were still dinners to prepare.

He rarely encountered his own Kind out here in the deeply wooded mountains, though legend had it that they had begun in a place very much like this—in remote, craggy Eastern Europe, far from where he now found himself. In other times he had lived, and worked and fed, much closer to that place. Sebastien had traveled everywhere, been to virtually every resort hotel on three continents; he had landed positions at most. Perhaps when his tenure here was over he would go back in the direction of Transylvania, or whatever today's cartographers called that old, wild country. He gathered that times there had lately changed—for half a century past, the resort business in those parts had been too slow to make them worth a visit. He did not care one way or the other about Communism, except that it retarded tourism so much.

He relied on steady business wherever he went. A busy resort employed more people, and he had been able to convince most managers to employ him too. He was, after all, a classically trained chef—"in the manner of Escoffier," he could assure them, and they would never know how many of his recipes came directly from the master's own hand-scrawled notebooks. But more importantly, he needed a ceaseless flow of guests. From his post in the well-appointed kitchen, he could look out at the evening's diners, holding spoonfuls of his lobster bisque or forkfuls of his coq au vin to their ruddy mouths, and, if he were hungry, decide whom he would choose.

When another of his Blood appeared, it always came as a surprise, for their visits could not be predicted—but it also made a certain sense. Each of them had to situate himself or herself in a place with available prey, yet with enough coming and going that he or she would not be discovered. Sebastien chose to live at resorts; others of his Kind chose to patronize them. Ironically, they were the only guests who were not in a position to praise his cooking, though doubtless they had enjoyed its savor in the blood of some hapless diner whom they surprised on his or her postprandial stroll.

Chefcraft had come very easily to Sebastien. He had dined well and heartily when he lived as a human man, before the Blood; he had been a gourmand, why not admit it, with enough extra money to satiate his hungers well. He looked back on those days with nostalgia: hunger today was not so simple, satiation not so certain. But the Blood had given him abilities that dovetailed well with his old appetites, so that, while eating food was out of the question, his powers of smell let him create extraordinary dishes, nuanced, finely spiced. He had never left a position because they did not like his work—and rarely because they suspected him of anything unsavory. No, he left of his own accord, usually, because, never showing age, he could not stay more than a decade or so in any one place without arousing curiosity. And curiosity, he knew full well, was the mother of suspicion.

He had lived and worked up here, high in the alpine Rockies, for seven years. The diners who peopled his beautifully rustic hall, clinking glasses and exclaiming over his dishes, were, excited chef's assistants told him, producers and movie stars. He didn't care about that, though once he understood how high-profile those potential victims were, he avoided them. Few looked delicious enough to be worth the risk of exposure, should he effect one's disappearance.

Tonight his dining room was half-full, and he had already asked the gossipy salad-boy to point out the famous ones to him. Thank god the one who stood out to him was a blank, anonymous face to the star-struck kitchen help. It had been weeks since Sebastien had fed—but years since he had seen a man who made him so deeply, achingly hungry. On the deck, gazing down into the ravine, he mulled his strategy. He guessed this one would be simple to harvest—the man had already locked eyes with Sebastien across the dining room, and, seeing Sebastien in his chef's toque, raised a soup spoon in salute. His eyes lingered on Sebastien, too, and that was what would make pursuit so easy.

Pleasurable, too; one could always feed on a victim taken by surprise, and one could often seduce him into compliance. But nothing matched the feeling of taking someone who wanted to be taken…even if the taking he had thought he wanted was more prosaic, and both more and less carnal, than what he got.

Pursuit was hardly the word an outsider watching them would choose, however. As soon as the evening's last dinner had been plated, Sebastien removed his apron and toque, and ran his hands through his dark curly hair. Stepping into the dining room, he saw that the man sat still at his window table, looking out into the black night. He held a glass of port—a very rich old port, Sebastien knew by the scent. The remaining diners, the serving staff moving about, the tables and the leaping fire in the stone fireplace all reflected in the window as he approached the table—everything appeared there except Sebastien.

But the man heard him approach and turned.

"You've enjoyed your meal?" Sebastien asked, standing rather formally next to the beautiful man's table. At this range his scent was intoxicating, mingled as it was with old tawny port and with the pale scent of the dinner Sebastien had cooked and he had eaten.

"Very much, sir," said the diner. "It was fabulous. I haven't eaten this well in years."

"Gratifying," said Sebastien. "I hoped it had pleased you."

"Sir, would you care to join me in a glass of port? Please let me introduce myself—I'm David. And you'd be Monsieur Sebastien?" At Sebastien's surprised look, David hastened, "You're the head chef, are you not? You are named on the menu."

"Ah, certainly," murmured Sebastien. "Yes, I'd be pleased to sit down. You're here alone?" His eyes, only his eyes, could feed on David, for whom he was suddenly dizzyingly hungry, and when the blond diner offered his hand, he lingered over it. He was rewarded with a gift he could feel, though not yet taste: David offering himself up. It happened on the energy plane only, when David smiled and said, "Yes, quite alone—until this moment," and the blood surged in his veins so that Sebastien could almost see it, sang to him with a hum he could hear.

They sat at the table for a few more minutes, making small talk, though little enough of it considering they had only met. Sebastien disliked the very chatty ones; he could feel the spirit fighting its knowledge of who he was, and this was off-putting—affected the flavor of the blood, too, which was worse. David, though, was with him almost quietly. Until he'd paid, counted out his change, left a tip, and said, "Would you like to go?"

Sebastien had been in every one of the old stone hotel's pine-paneled rooms. David was staying in his favorite—the one up in the eaves. Lying on the bed, one looked up into a log-beamed, vaulted ceiling with hand-hewn rafters, and there was a triangular window whose point extended all the way up to the ceiling's peak. The bed itself was carved of small logs—it was sturdy enough to cradle the most vigorous lovemaking, even to contain a man in his death-throes. Sebastien did not always view his prey as lovers, to be sure. But David would be one of those few exceptions—angel to his demon, causing Sebastien's usually cool flesh to warm.

David bolted the door and turned to him, eyes burning. "Sebastien, I don't know you. It might not matter to you if I tell you I rarely act this way, rarely feel like this. I don't even care what you're into. Please, whatever you like to do, do it to me now."

Sebastien had to do everything, usually—seduce, subdue. Now he could order what he wanted, as if from a menu. Which appetizer did he want first? "David, take off your clothes," he said, and stood before the great triangular window, and watched.

David did more than he was asked; he stripped naked, then came to Sebastien and knelt before him. His cock was hard and high, and seeing it, Sebastien yearned to wrap his tongue around it, swallow it down. His feelings, too, were unusual; he usually thought of nothing except their blood, how much he would take, whether or not to leave them enough to sleep the night away and waken shakily in the morning, never remembering.

In the room's low light, Sebastien didn't hesitate to tear off his own clothes, revealing a body so finely white and beautifully muscled that David gasped and laid both warm hands on him. "Sebastien, you're so cold!" he cried when he touched the flesh that felt more statue than human, and Sebastien pulled him up, saying, "Shhh, you will warm me."

On the bed, then, kissing and tussling; rubbing his cool body against David's flushed one, Sebastien felt his own cock pulse and grow—a sensation so rare to him that he scarcely remembered when he had last felt it. Most of his feedings bore little resemblance to human lovemaking. But when the Blood filled his tool, he used it, and the knowledge that he would use it tonight suffused his hunger with something finer and hotter. David filled his arms, rubbing his body urgently against Sebastien, hot human blood scented with port and lust and the spices Sebastien had used to stew the rabbit David had eaten for dinner.

Had David felt the teeth yet, scraping into the kiss, palpable even when his mouth was closed? The blond man was in a swoon in his arms, and it had only to do with the sexual heat he felt and his desire to be taken by Sebastien—he had not yet lost a drop of that highly scented blood. But in a moment Sebastien would begin. He pinned David to the bed, the muscular human man no match at all for his ancient strength, and rubbed cock on cock ferociously as he leaned into David to whisper, "Remember what you told me. You're safe with me unless you fight me."

Then he began to bite.

Tiny punctures, nothing more. Enough to release little trickles of David's sweet, spicy blood, but certainly not enough to truly hurt him. Sebastien bit down carefully, sharp fangs entering David's body everywhere and his long tongue lapping after the teeth had drawn the blood. Even a tiny taste of it made him quake; when he really fed, he would have to be scrupulously careful not to maim David. It was so easy to lose control.

The rills of blood welled up from David's cheek, his throat, his chest, his thighs. They collected in hollows, carmine pools that made Sebastien shake. Turning David over, Sebastien cut through the meaty globe of one asscheek, and the lick that followed earned an especially guttural moan. Sebastien let the small puncture bleed for a moment, the rivulet running into the cleft of David's ass, then let his tongue prowl after it. David's moans grew louder: he would fuck him, Sebastien decided then, but first he turned him over to savor the warm, rigid cock.

Sebastien hadn't sucked cock for a very long time. It wasn't wise, even when he left his prey dead, to leave them mutilated, and in the throes of feeding, he could not always stop himself from biting completely through. But tonight he floated on a haze of sex, not just hunger, and he bit David's prick only a little, gnawed it like a sausage, licked it and sucked. Blood ebbed rhythmically out of the small wounds he made, mingled with David's precum, tasting extra salty, savory. He didn't let David ejaculate, but made him ride the intense arousal: a little pain, a lot of physical ecstasy. Then there was the emotion he could taste with the blood, something like love, an intensely felt submission that David rode like a drug high. It was not a craving for annihilation—Sebastien knew that flavor, and it was nothing so rich as this. It was not even a desire for the Blood, not exactly, though he knew David would take It from him as he would anything else.

David was making sounds, no, trying to make words. Sebastien finally made them out, guttural pleas of "Let me...let me taste you..." It dawned on Sebastien that David wanted his cock. He knelt over the man to let him have it, letting David's mouth fill, the strange silk of his balls covering David's nose. To thrill David more than to please himself, he sat back a little, cutting off David's air. He was rewarded by a deep groan in which he read more erotic pleasure than had been shown by anyone he had dallied with since he came into the Blood. In the hot, close, sucking mouth, Sebastien's cock jumped and grew big.

It would not be possible to come from David's cocksucking, no matter how ardent or skillful. He usually found it impossible to come at all, excepting the orgasmic shudder that overcame him with a rush of hot, living blood. But tonight he would have both. He let David work his cock for a few minutes—it excited the man so, Sebastien could smell it. The hot tongue worked his balls, his asshole, everything it could reach, but finally Sebastien could wait no longer.

He lifted his body off David's and pushed him roughly onto his belly—not because he felt rough, no, in fact he felt incredibly tender, but because he read the high arousal that awaited harsh treatment. The trickle of blood from David's asscheek had subsided, but it was still wet where Sebastien wanted it: his lover's asshole. Using the barely slick liquid as lube, he rammed in. David screamed, as much from heat as pain, and whimpered words again as Sebastien began to stroke: "Take me, yes, please, open me, please, take my ass..." At these words—and the powerful scent that emanated from them—the Blood-engorged cock swelled and leaped. Sebastien felt the fire of David's guts around him, soft and hot, the muscular ring of anus tight. What never happened would happen tonight: David would milk him.

But even this fuck would not be enough. Sebastien clasped David's chest in his arms, lifting him half off the bed like a rag doll, a carcass. With one hand he gently turned the man's head—his teeth were singing with urgency, seeking a place to bite. The soft neck drew them the way his cock had been drawn to plunge into that asshole.

But there was nothing, no feeling in all the dimensions, like this: cock still pumping, more sensitized than he had ever felt it, and teeth tearing at the flesh, the blood coming, his mouth filling. This fuck was total, as his teeth pierced, as his cock drove in, as David screamed—and what he screamed was "Yes!" The man's blood welled up like a fountain. Sebastien drank, he held David close, and he fucked into the blood-slicked ass like the demon he so surely was.

David would remember this fuck, if he lived, but not how long it went on—Sebastien could warp time like spaghetti, and perhaps he went on for hours coupling with the man, a fuck that sliced Death into Life like a sharp blade entering and withdrawing. He could not, would not, kill David, but neither could he stop fucking until the Blood in his cock had its own satiation. This came long after he had stopped drinking, even after he had ceased much movement into David's hole. They had lain together barely moving, and Sebastien lapped at David's wounds now to heal them, like a cat licks an injured paw. David keened and whimpered barely audibly—but he was alive. His soul floated somewhere Sebastien could barely see, but it had not disconnected from the man.

Sebastien came because David spoke to him, perhaps not with his voice, saying, "Yours, I am yours." It was still no desire for oblivion. It was still the richly scented submission it had been before Sebastien had opened David's veins. Sebastien's cock began pumping again, more fiercely than before, almost without Sebastien's will. With one arm, he held David to his heart. With the other, he took the man's cock, stroked it just like a human would do. And as jets of cum spurted out of David's cock, filling Sebastien's hand, his own deep hunger sated, he gave a yell and released everything into David's guts. It seemed he would never stop pumping his jism into the man's ass—how long had it been? Two hundred years? Three?

Floating with David on a cloud of release, Sebastien felt the nearest thing to bliss he had known since the moment the Blood took him.

He wished it were possible for David to pin him down, tear his throat out, and drink.

Waiting for the Vampire

WILLIAM J. MANN

"There is a very good reason I have not allowed myself to die, not for nearly a hundred years," said old Mr. Samuel Horowitz, the oldest man at the Hebrew Home.

"And what's that, Mr. Horowitz?"

"It's because when I was a young boy in Russia, back in the days of the tsars, I was bitten by a vampire, and now I am afraid to die." He opened his eyes wide. "I am afraid that when I die, I will rise from my grave as one of the undead."

Ogden Smith, twenty-five and new to his job at the Hebrew Home, wasn't expecting this. Mr. Horowitz was a strange man, and he had been known to grope the male aides in places he might never touch the females, but Ogden Smith was not expecting talk of vampires. He was sitting next to the old man, who was one hundred and six, and he had just finished pouring him a cup of tea.

"Oh, Mr. Horowitz," Ogden said at last, not knowing what else to say.

"You don't believe me." The old man shifted in his chair, as easily as a hundred-and-six-year-old man could, and looked out the window. It was a cold January day, and the snow had drifted high, covering the bottoms of the dusty panes of glass. It was very white outside, and Samuel Horowitz's old brown eyes blinked against the brightness.

"The light hurts my eyes, you know," he said finally. "Has ever since." He sighed. "No one has ever believed me," he lamented, in that odd guttural Russian accent of his.

Ogden offered a small, timid laugh. "There aren't such things as vampires," he said. "Here, drink your tea."

"You think not?" the old man said, turning on him with all the ferocity of a child denied. "You are wrong. In Russia, there were vampires. And one of them came to my home. Invited by my father, in fact. They must be invited, you know. They cannot enter a place unbidden. His name was Count Alexei Petrovich Guchkov. He was a most charming man. Tall and handsome and dark. I was just sixteen. My father had money. They all hated my father because he was a Jew, but he had money, so they tolerated him. At least for a little while. Count Guchkov would come to our house and my mother would offer him wine, but he would always refuse. I found him mesmerizing. I could not take my eyes off him."

"Mr. Horowitz..." Ogden was growing uncomfortable with such talk of mesmerizing men.

"What? Will you tell me it was merely a schoolboy fancy? That he forced himself upon me, or that perhaps somehow I wanted it? Well, I did. One night, on our terrace, on a cold black winter night, with the moon in the sky and the snow anxious to fall, he put his warm lips on mine and kissed me, deep and hard, with my parents just a few feet away, not knowing..."

"Oh, please, Mr. Horowitz..."

"He kissed me, Mr. Smith, and I liked it. He awoke in me passions I had forgotten from another life, passions that I have never felt since. His lips were warm but his hands were cold, and that was all right by me, especially when he moved his hands down my neck and over my shoulders, down between my legs..."

"Oh..."

"And then he pulled me into him, his strong arms wrapped around me, and I surrendered, willingly, eagerly, as he sunk his teeth into my throat and drank my young virgin blood."

Mr. Horowitz was quiet. He let out a deep, long, labored breath and resumed looking out the window. Ogden Smith said nothing. He just sat there, breathing. Finally, with trembling fingers, he lifted Mr. Horowitz's cup of tea to his own lips, and drank.

"I want to have my hair cut short, like Elizabeth Taylor's," Bernadette Smith told her brother.

"That would be attractive," Ogden agreed.

"Chase just adores Elizabeth Taylor. More than Kim Novak now. Remember when all he could talk about was Kim Novak?"

"Yes," Ogden said.

"We're going away, you know," Bernadette said, still looking at herself in the mirror. Her brother sat behind her, at the foot of her bed.

"You are? Oh, Bernie, when?" There was some degree of panic in his voice.

"On Tuesday. Just for three days." She looked at her brother in the mirror. "Now don't start. I'm twenty-six years old, Og. I've wasted enough time."

Ogden knew better than to debate his sister. He waited a few minutes, until Bernie had moved away from the mirror and stood in front of the window, pulling on her hose.

"So where are you going?" he asked.

"We're going on an *airplane!*" Bernadette said, wide-eyed and big-mouthed, and for a moment Ogden wanted to slap her, but then pushed the thought away.

"An airplane?"

"Yes. To get away from all this cold and snow. We're going to St. Croix! It's in the Virgin Islands. We own it. The United States, I mean."

"Yes, I've heard of it."

"Can you just imagine, Og? White sandy beaches and a big sun overhead. And the water's so crystal blue and clear you can see the brightly colored tropical fish." She paused, as if expecting her brother to voice disbelief. "It says so, in the brochure."

Ogden smiled.

"Isn't it just too divine? It was Chase's idea. He's paying for the whole thing! He got a deal, a special midweek deal, through the travel agency he works for." Bernie flopped down on the bed next to her brother, clutching the pillow to her chest and squeezing it. "Wasn't I lucky to find him?"

"Yes," Ogden said, standing up and going to the mirror himself.

He discovered her eyes. They stared back at him like big black balls, like the eight balls Papa used to shoot down at the pool hall.

"Bernie," he asked, not turning around, "do you believe in vampires?"

But his sister had left the room. To start packing, no doubt.

"It was the year 1868," Mr. Horowitz told him the next day when he again brought him some tea. "Ever since then, I have been determined to stay alive."

"That is a good thing," Ogden told him. "You have lived a long and eventful life."

"A *good* thing? My young friend, would you want to live a life of such fear? The fear every night that grips you, the fear that when you go to sleep, you will not wake, until one cold night you awake in your coffin, the lust for blood overpowering you?"

"Please, Mr. Horowitz, please don't start talking that way again..."

"When I saw you the first day you were here, I thought maybe you might believe me, that you weren't like the others."

Ogden Smith, standing over the old man's bed, looked down at him with his eyes, not moving his chin.

"I thought there was a chance you might believe," Mr. Horowitz pouted.

"Vampires aren't real," Ogden said firmly.

"Count Guchkov was. I can still feel the warmth of his mouth and the coldness of his hands, here," he said, placing his right hand over his crotch, beneath the flimsy white sheet.

Ogden Smith turned away. "Do you want some honey for your tea?"

"Are you Christian, Mr. Smith?"

Ogden turned back to face him. "Yes."

"And you work here, as an aide in the Hebrew Home?"

"Yes."

"That is why I noticed the difference. The Jews have stopped believing in such things. We have seen too much horror at the hands of men to believe in such things as vampires anymore. But we believed once. Have you ever heard the story of the Golem, Mr. Smith?"

"No, Mr. Horowitz, and please, don't tell me. You frighten me."

The old man moved his head against his pillow. He still had thick white hair, loose around his face, a face of old bark, of a thousand crevices, of years of pain and anguish and scattered moments of joy, but mostly of fear.

"Frighten you?" he sighed. "I do not mean to. Yet fear is the great equalizer, my friend. What kind of Christian are you?"

"What kind?"

"Yes. Are you Anglican? Catholic?"

"Lutheran."

"Ah. The German Protestant." Mr. Horowitz closed his eyes. "They hunted us down, but that was many years later. I was living with my sister and her husband then. I had never married, of course.

Who would want me? I had been defiled. We had been driven from Russia by the Communists, but Germany wasn't far enough away to save me from a vampire. He still haunted my dreams. He could have found me, come to me, drank my blood again, if he had so chosen."

"Mr. Horowitz…"

"So leave if you don't want to hear! Why do you stand there, if what I tell you so disturbs you?"

"I'm concerned that you may be upsetting yourself."

"Upsetting myself!" The old man turned his head away from Ogden Smith. "I have felt this way for ninety years, as I hid not only from the Russians and the Germans but also from a creature of the night who was even more loathsome. I have feared death because of what it could mean to me. When the Germans forced us out, when in the black of night my brother-in-law huddled us under blankets and drove us to a waiting train so we could escape to America, I rejoiced. For so long I had wanted to come here, for only here, across the ocean, across the moving waters, would I be safe." He paused and looked hard at Ogden. "You see, a vampire cannot cross moving water."

Ogden had sat down in the chair beside the old man's bed. "But yet you are still afraid," he said.

The old man closed his eyes. "Yes. There is no escape. He could not get to me here, but in my blood his taint remains. That has never left me. And when I die…"

"Mr. Horowitz, please don't say it…"

"I can't go on living forever! It has been an act of sheer will to live this long. I have kept death at arm's length for nearly a century. I have refused to open the door when he came courting, and he has come many times, Mr. Smith, many times. But I grow tired. I cannot continue much longer. And when I die, Mr. Smith…"

"Yes? What will happen when you die?"

"…on the night of the third day, I will arise, out of my grave, a vampire myself, returned to feast on the blood of the living, one of the undead."

Ogden Smith had put his hands to his mouth. He could not speak.

"Hey, stop that!"

Bernadette was standing in front of the mirror again, wearing nothing but her black bra and red panties. Chase, her rich young boyfriend, was on his hands and knees on the bed behind her. He had snapped the back of her bra strap so that it made a sharp sound slapping against her flesh.

Ogden had been passing in the hall, and now paused in the doorway. "Are you all right, Bernie?" he asked.

"Sure. Hey, Og," Bernie called.

"Yes?"

"You sure you'll be all right here by yourself while we're gone?"

Chase laughed. " 'Course he will. Og's a big boy, honey. Ain't ya now, Og?"

Ogden looked at him. "I'll be fine," he said.

"Sure you will, Oggie kid," Chase said, pouncing off the bed and coming at him. He put his hands on Ogden's hips and gave him a quick kiss on the nose. Ogden hated it when Chase did things like that, but he didn't pull away.

"You just need to remember a few things," Bernadette was saying, pulling on her lacy white blouse and buttoning it down the front, the black bra showing through. "Freddie, the paper boy, needs to get paid on Thursday. I've left the money in an envelope. And Mr. Otfinowski, the milk man, he gets paid on Friday morning. Make sure you leave his money in the crate Thursday night, because otherwise he comes so early you'll never catch him. We'll be coming back Friday afternoon, but by the time Chase's brother picks us up at the airport and we grab some dinner, it might be late."

"That's fine," Ogden said.

Chase was still in his face. "Gosh, you've got pretty eyes," he said suddenly.

Ogden yanked away and hurried down the hall to his room. He could hear his sister shushing Chase, saying he shouldn't have said that. "But I never noticed," he said, "till just then. They're so *green.*" That's when Ogden turned the radio on quite loud, singing along in his head with Bobby Darin to "Mack the Knife."

The Smith siblings lived in an old flat in a building on Pleasant Street, just off Main, one of the grand old buildings in town, with the elegant moldings of the nineteenth century. Despite its years, it was a clean building, and good, decent families still lived there: families with names like Wright, and Russell, and Williams. Only one immigrant family lived there, and they on the topmost floor: the

Trykowskis, a Polish man and his second wife and their three teenaged daughters.

Mr. Otfinowski, the milk man, was Polish too, but he lived down by the great bend of the river, with the other Polish and Italian families. Ogden liked Mr. Otfinowski a great deal. "Top o' the morning to you," he'd say like an Irishman. It always made Ogden laugh. From his window he could see the top of the next building, and the next, and just beyond that the steeple of St. John the Baptist, the Catholic church on Main Street. Sometimes, atop one of the buildings, he'd spy some kids in the summertime, sun bathing, the girls seemingly always on one side of the steeple, the boys on the other. Of course, it was too cold for sunbathing now, so Ogden didn't even bother to look. Sometimes, instead, he'd look out the window in the other direction, up the hill toward the orchard, where the great houses stood. That's where his father had been born, in one of those houses: he'd pointed it out to Ogden when he was about ten. But Papa had married a Catholic girl, and Grandfather had been very angry, and booted poor Papa all the way down that great hill. That's why they ended up here.

Tonight Ogden was thinking about vampires, and wondered if he'd ever been frightened of such things before. No, he didn't think so, but he couldn't be sure. He had seen a vampire movie years ago—with Papa, he thought, and surely he would have reassured him that such things were not real. There was another vampire movie now, playing at the Palace on Main Street, something with a man named Lee. Ogden had seen the ads for it in the paper. But he certainly had no plans to see it. How silly, he chided himself, pulling his blankets up to his chin as he lay there in the dark. How silly I'm being.

He heard his sister moan. Tomorrow she would be gone: for four whole days and three nights. And Chase with her.

"Oh, God," Bernie gushed suddenly from her room, and Ogden turned his face to the wall.

"Yeah, that's it, baby," Chase said, and Ogden wasn't sure if he actually heard him, or if his words were merely inside his head, a memory from other times like this.

He flung back the covers and placed his bare feet against the cold hardwood floor.

"Ohhhh," his sister groaned through the wall.

The flat was utterly dark. In the winter, with the windows closed, the rooms were as quiet as they were dark. Ogden could lie in bed and listen to Mr. Trykowski's old pendulum clock strike the hour from two floors above. Then their own clock would chime: one o'clock, two o'clock, three o'clock, all through the night.

He knew the blueprint of the flat; scuffing in the darkness was easy. He padded into the hallway, and a small flickering light shone from the crack between his sister's door and its frame. That tiny little sliver of light, cast from a candle by the side of the bed, was enough to let Ogden see just a little: the heaving of Chase's strong muscular bare back, the red-tipped hands of his sister laced around his neck. He watched soundlessly for several moments before turning away.

Ogden walked into the dark bathroom, the tiles of the floor even colder than the wood, his feet reacting, wanting to run. But he stood above the toilet, effortlessly reaching down and finding the handle in the dark. He flushed.

The sound of the water rushing through the pipes in the great old building echoed among the rooms, as surely as they must have in each of the flats in the building. Somewhere above them, perhaps Mr. Trykowski sat up in his bed and wondered who was awake at this hour. Below them, maybe old Miss Wright, who had taught them in kindergarten, woke from a sound sleep and shook her head in dismay.

When Ogden left the bathroom, he knew the sliver of shivering light from his sister's room would be gone, and the sounds would have stopped.

He was right.

Mr. Horowitz died the morning Bernadette and Chase got on their airplane and flew to St. Croix.

"Oh, no," Ogden Smith said, arriving at the Hebrew Home.

Mrs. Newberg nodded. "Poor old war horse. He didn't want to go. He fought like an old tiger right to the end."

"This was this morning?"

"Yes. Very early. Before the sun was up. That was why he was fighting so, trying to hold back."

"I don't understand," said Ogden Smith.

"He said he wanted to see the sun, one last time," Mrs. Newberg explained.

"Oh," said Ogden.

"Very sad, really. But he'd lived a long time. A very long time. You were close to him, weren't you?"

But Ogden Smith wasn't listening. Somewhere overhead, an airplane passed, and it seemed as if the building shook.

The movie was the *Horror of Dracula,* and there was a big sign for it underneath the marquee of the Palace. At night, light bulbs around the sign were lit up, just like the lights up on the marquee. As a child, Ogden had loved coming to the Palace when it was all lit up, and he'd be there to see the latest Deanna Durbin picture, or Andy Hardy, or anything with Lana Turner. He and Bernie would troop down from their home, their father urging Bernie to hold Og's hand. "And come right home after the picture," he'd admonish them.

"Yes, Papa," they both would promise.

Only once did they disobey, and then Ogden got a spanking. They had stopped to talk with a boy from Bernie's class, a boy named Walter Moriarty, an Irish kid with red hair and lots of freckles and bowed legs. All the girls thought he was the cutest boy in the school. Bernie had the biggest crush on him of any of the girls. Ogden couldn't quite figure out why, but he secretly wished his hair was as red as Walter's, that he had freckles all over his face, too. When Walter called over to them, of course they had stopped. Walter was eating a chocolate bar and he asked if Bernie wanted a bite. Ogden wanted so much to taste the candy himself, but of course Walter would never ask him. Bernie had looked down at Ogden, who glared up at her with hard little nine-year-old eyes. "That'd be swell," Bernie had said, daringly, and Walter had held the candy bar in front of her face. She took a bite, right on the spot he had bitten himself just moments before, and she smiled broadly. "That tastes good," she boasted.

Later, at home, when Papa had asked why they were late, Ogden had gleefully squealed. "Bernie stopped to talk with a boy and she took a bite of the candy bar he was eating," he shrieked. Papa's face had turned red and he yanked Bernie without saying a word across his knee and beat her until she cried. Ogden got it next, for squealing. Then Papa stormed out of the house, not returning until the next day.

"Do you like vampire movies?"

Ogden was startled by the voice. He looked up from the poster and saw a man standing next to him, an older man, very distinguished looking, much like the man in the movie poster, an actor whose name, he thought, was Cushing.

"Oh, I was simply—"

He felt his voice catch in his throat. The sun was setting. Bernie should have arrived in St. Croix by now.

"It's quite good," the man was saying. "But of course, there is so much more they are allowed to show on the screen these days. The Lugosi version was much tamer, but I think better. Have you seen it?"

He had a slight British accent, or at least Ogden thought he did. "No," he said. "Well, I don't remember. It's possible."

"And here I thought you were a vampire fan," he said.

"Oh, no," he said. "No, I'm not."

"Just curious then?"

"Yes." He made a polite smile. "Excuse me."

"The show is starting in a few minutes. Would you care to join me?"

"No," Ogden replied, too harshly, backing away. "No," he said again, catching himself, not wanting to appear impolite. "But thank you." He hurried away.

The town at night was a blur of colors. The red and blue neon of Main Street shops and restaurants flashed on and off, and the streetlamps poured pale yellow light onto the street. It was a Tuesday night, not a busy night, but still, couples strolled arm-in-arm, perhaps on their way to the movies, or to dinner. A gaggle of little girls in Girl Scout uniforms tagged behind an older woman, perhaps on their way home after a meeting. Ogden watched them as they crossed the street and all climbed into the back of a big black station wagon. To Ogden, it looked like a hearse.

"Oh, stop," he scolded himself. But as the shadows lengthened and the light blue of twilight melted in the deep purple of the evening, he dreaded returning to the empty flat. He sat there on the bench, facing the traffic of Main Street, lulled by the motion of the green and white buses and the golden orange of the taxicab lights, and fought against the tide of sleep that was trying to claim him. The bustle of people on the sidewalk behind him kept him awake, if not alert. Finally, overcome, he stood wearily, and walked up the two blocks to his home.

He had considered sitting shiva for old Mr. Horowitz at the Hebrew Home, but something seemed not right about that. Not because he was a Christian, he told himself, but because Mr. Horowitz wasn't really dead: no, the corpse they had placed in the mausoleum this very day was just waiting, waiting for three nights from now, waiting to claw its way through the satin lining of the coffin and break free of its prison.

"Stop this nonsense," Ogden Smith told himself, and he placed both his hands down on the formica top of the kitchen table and closed his eyes very tightly. "Stop this nonsense right now, Ogden Albert Smith."

When he opened them, he heard music: strange tinny music, as if from an old phonograph, somewhere in the building. It disturbed him, but he wasn't sure why. He opened the door of the old Kelvinator and removed a glass jar of milk. Unscrewing the cap, he poured himself a glass, and allowed his eyes to wander through the gray kitchen. Behind the dull glass of the cupboard sat the old china with its faded blue flower pattern, the china that had been his mother's. Or so Papa had said. He decided they should use the china more: it was better than their old brown plates, which were getting chipped now and were shameful to serve to company. Even to Chase.

And the flat needed painting, Ogden decided. When was the last time it had been painted? Papa had painted it last, at least fifteen years ago, when he and Bernie had both been children. It had been egg-shell white then: he remembered the name on the paint can. Now it was just gray: everything was gray.

The tinny music seemed to have grown louder. Ogden placed his glass in the sink. He wished the music would die down; how would he sleep? He supposed he could tap on Miss Wright's door, but it probably wasn't her. It could be one of Mr. Trykowski's daughters: except they played rock 'n' roll, and only on Saturdays, when their parents were out grocery shopping. He wasn't sure who could be playing this music: it seemed old, very old, as if it were coming from a Victrola—

"Stop it," he said to himself. He had flashed on an image: Mr. Horowitz as a young boy in Russia, with the great noble Count Alexei Petrovich Guchkov bent over, kissing his hand, a Victrola in the background, playing this very same music. "Stop it," he repeated out loud, and his words made a curious echo in the kitchen. "Victrolas probably weren't even invented in 1868."

49

He went into Bernadette's bedroom and sat down on her neatly made bed. "Just three days," he whispered to himself, staring at his reflection in the mirror. "Just three nights," he heard another voice say, inside him. And in the glass, he thought he saw old Mr. Horowitz, chalk white face and blood red lips, rising up from behind him on the bed.

"But that would not be possible," the man was saying. "Vampires cast no reflection."

"It was in my mind," Ogden explained, not wanting him to think he was crazy. He couldn't be crazy if he *knew* he had imagined it.

"It is all patently impossible," the man said with finality, and Ogden wished he had never mentioned it. He hadn't wanted the man to take him seriously.

They had met again, quite by chance, at the counter of Henry's, where Lois had just served Ogden a grilled cheese and a cup of tea. He had stopped here for lunch, as he often did, since the Hebrew Home was just up the block, on Washington Street.

"Ah, my vampire friend," the man had said, sitting down on the stool next to him. The restaurant was not that crowded; there were other places he could have sat.

He said hello. He introduced himself. "I'm Stanley Kowalski," he said, then grinned: "Not *that* Stanley Kowalski." In fact, he said, his name was Stanislaus: he'd been born in Poland, but his parents came to America when he was just ten months old. He'd been Stanley ever since.

"Might I inquire as to your name?" he asked, in a gallant sort of way.

"Smith," he said. "Ogden Smith."

"Well, Mr. Smith, if I in any way offended you the other day, allow me to apologize."

Ogden smiled a little. "No, there's no need to apologize. I was simply—" He paused. "A man I knew had just passed away. I was a bit out of sorts."

And so he told him the story of Mr. Samuel Horowitz.

Stanley Kowalski took a long sip of his coffee. "No, it's not possible," he said.

"Of course it's not," Ogden agreed, wishing he had never shared this with him, with this man, this total stranger. He wanted to pay and leave. He wasn't hungry anymore. He tried to get Lois' attention, but she was pouring some more coffee for a man at the other end of the counter.

"I'll tell you why it's not possible. For a vampire to create another in his image, he must first kill his victim. If what Mr. Horowitz says is true, this Russian Count forgot about him, as vampires must do the majority of their victims, otherwise we'd be overrun with the creatures. The vampiric taint wears off, I assume. One would only become a vampire if the taint is in their blood at the time of their death, which would mean, that they die of a vampire attack itself. Think of the Dracula story, my boy. Mina Harker was not going to turn into a vampire when she died. Poor Miss Lucy, on the other hand—she became a creature of the night because the Count sucked her dry, so to speak, and killed her."

Ogden Smith was shocked. It showed on his face.

"I'm sorry," Mr. Kowalski said at once. "Have I offended you?"

"I suppose I brought it on myself," he said, taking a breath. "I brought the horrible subject up."

"Are you all right? May I walk you home?"

"I'm fine," he insisted, sliding off of his stool. "I've got to get back to work anyway."

"Let me pay for your lunch," Stanley Kowalski offered.

"No, no, absolutely not," he said. He handed two dollar bills across the counter to Lois. "Keep the change," he said hurriedly. Lois waved without turning around from the cash register. "Good afternoon, Mr. Kowalski," Ogden said, and rushed out the door.

In Mr. Horowitz's room that day, just as the sun began to sink lower in the sky, Ogden helped the other aides pack up the dead man's belongings. There was no family. Some of the personal items would be distributed among the other residents. The rest would be discarded.

There was a small icon of the Virgin Mary in Mr. Horowitz's jewelry box, along with a silver Star of David, its points still very shiny and quite sharp. Relics from the motherland, he supposed. Yet how odd that the Christian icon should be there as well.

"No one here will want *that,*" said Mavis, a colored aide. "Do you think I could have it?"

Ogden wasn't sure. "We should ask Mrs. Newberg."

Mavis made a face. "She'll say no. Come on, Ogden. Who'll care?"

"All right," he said, handing over the icon to Mavis. She grinned when she got it, and her eyes danced.

That left the Star of David. Ogden stared at it for a few moments. Then he slipped it into his pocket. Who'll care?

The sun edged the horizon.

Two more nights.

He hoped he would sleep better tonight. How quiet the flat was. He had always known it was quiet, and had learned to live with it. He actually preferred the quiet to Bernie's moans and groans, which had started about eight months ago, when Chase had first come into their lives. Until then, there had been no men. They'd eat their meals together, maybe see a picture, maybe go down to Miss Wright's, their old kindergarten teacher, and watch her television set. She had been the first in the building to buy one, but now the Trykowskis had one, too. The Smith siblings had still not purchased a set.

Then Chase arrived. He was the brother of one of Bernie's pupils in her second-grade class. Bernie taught at the Edna Stillman School off Washington Street, just as Papa had hoped she would. Papa had saved all the money he made from the pool hall to send his children to college: Ogden to the Marcus T. Wilson School of Business and Bernadette to the State Teachers' School. But only Bernie had completed her studies: Ogden had left school after the first trimester. He preferred not to think about that.

Instead, he worked as an aide. First at St. Luke's, the Lutheran home, for a couple of years, where he tended to his own kind. But he never got a raise, and the Hebrew Home paid better wages. So just a few months ago, he had summoned all his courage and told the matron at St. Luke's that he was giving his notice, and two weeks later began his new career at the Hebrew Home, making thirty-five cents an hour more. The change prompted applause from Bernie. "Well," she'd smiled, "wouldn't Papa be proud of how you asserted yourself."

But Ogden wondered if Papa would be as proud of Bernie. She had changed a great deal since she met Chase. Ogden thought it highly improper that she was dating the older brother of one of her pupils. But people hadn't really started talking yet, or if they had, Ogden hadn't heard them. But now that it was winter break, Bernie and Chase were carrying on with much less discretion. Ogden hated to think what Papa would have said.

But tonight, sitting on Bernie's bed, there was some small part of him that would have traded the relentless quiet for the sounds of his sister's passion. On his lap he cradled a pillow—the one Chase had slept on, he thought, just two nights before. What he wanted to do, desperately, was push that pillow into his face and inhale, but he dared not. "Stop it," he scolded himself.

The music again. That same tinny music. From somewhere. Not above, not below. He flung the pillow to the floor and stood, pushing himself to the window and pressing his face up against the cold glass. The pane had fogged up too much to see outside. Where was the music *coming* from? What song did it play?

He paced the room. What time was it? Getting close to ten. He should go to sleep now. He had to be at the Hebrew Home by seven. Tomorrow was Thursday. Tomorrow he must pay the paper boy. And leave the money out for Mr. Otfinowski.

His stomach rumbled. "How silly of me," he said into the darkness. "I forgot to make myself dinner."

He stumbled into the kitchen and flicked on the overhead light. One of the bulbs had burned out; the glow was dim, not enough even to read by. He opened the cabinet next to the Kelvinator and considered a can of tuna fish. "It's too late to eat," he decided out loud, and closed the cabinet door.

At the window over the sink, something scratched at the glass. He jumped. "Oh!" he cried, and narrowed his eyes to see what was there.

Three long scratches scarred the frost; scratches like fingernails.

"A squirrel," he told himself. "A squirrel."

It couldn't be anything else: it hasn't been three nights—only two. And besides, Samuel Horowitz did not die from the bite of the vampire. The old man was wrong: the taint must have disappeared from his blood long ago. Ogden realized now that he had desperately tried to find some comfort in Mr. Kowalski's words. But Mr. Horowitz had been so sure, so sure he would rise again.

"Stop it," Ogden said to himself, turning out the light in the kitchen and quickly replacing it with the light in the hallway, which was brighter, more soothing. He passed by Bernie's room and turned into his own.

"I will sleep better tonight," he assured himself, getting undressed, "because last night I did not. I am tired enough tonight to fall asleep on a cold hard bench."

Standing there only in his underwear, long boxy polka-dotted shorts, looking at his plain round face in the mirror, he thought of the picture of his mother Papa had kept hidden among his handkerchiefs in his top drawer, in this very room that had once been his, when Ogden and Bernadette had shared the other room. Ogden used Papa's bureau now, but in his top drawer the photograph of his mother, in its little tin oval frame, was missing. It was burned long ago, shortly after Papa had died, when Ogden had tossed it, along with Papa's nightshirt, into the furnace.

The music kept Ogden awake, and the light he left burning beside the bed began to oppress him. At every little creak in the old building, he would start. Finally, he sat up, resting against his head board, and tried to read. It was one of Bernie's trashy novels, *Peyton Place,* but Ogden couldn't abide it for very long. He heard the Trykowskis' great clock chime twelve from the other corner of the building, and then the Smiths' own clock, out in the living room, also rang in the new day.

"Why should midnight mean anything more than any other time?" he asked out loud.

And suddenly he thought of the Jewish cemetery out near Devil's Hopyard, that strange field where scaly hops grew yellow in the summer, where the Indians first heard unaccountable noises centuries ago, where the early English settlers, Ogden's ancestors among them, had pronounced the land the devil's own. The noises, scientists would later say, were merely the rumblings of a minor fault far beneath the surface of the earth: but might they not instead be coming from hell, Ogden wondered now. The children of the town made up many stories regarding Devil's Hopyard, and sitting in bed this night, Ogden remembered them all. Worst of them were the tales of the cemeteries that ringed the hopyard: the flat, stark Jewish cemetery, where Mr. Horowitz's cold body lay in the mausoleum, waiting for the ground to thaw so he could be buried, and the hilly, ornate Protestant cemetery, where Ogden's mother had been interred these last twenty years.

"At night, the dead dance in Devil's Hopyard," Walter Moriarty had told them, and all the girls had squealed.

"Tell us more, Walter, tell us more!!"

"They crawl up out of their graves, the Jews and the Lutherans together, and they dance under the moon in the hopyard, to the sounds from the devil below," he'd intoned.

"No!"

Ogden covered his face with his hands. *Tell us no more,* Walter

Moriarty. I already know too much. Mr. Horowitz's body does not wait to be buried in the earth; it waits to walk again, to suck the blood of the living, to find virgin blood under a cold black winter sky, with the snow overhead, anxious to fall.

"I feel very foolish," Ogden Smith said to Stanley Kowalski.

"Please do not," he said.

They met at Henry's. Ogden had called him, having found his name in the phone book. Mr. Kowalski was only too happy to meet him for lunch. This time they got a booth. Ogden ordered a grilled cheese again. "The usual," Lois smiled, scribbling onto her pad. Mr. Kowalski ordered a steak burger with onions, very rare.

"I must get this out of my head," Ogden told him.

"After tonight, the fear will be gone," he assured him.

"I certainly hope so. I didn't sleep at all last night." He was sure he could tell. The black rings under his eyes revealed his secret.

"Even if Mr. Horowitz really *is* a vampire, and if tonight he *does* rise," he said, "there's no reason to believe he would come for you. And even if he did, Mr. Smith, vampires must first be *invited* into a home before they can enter. You are perfectly safe."

He didn't appear convinced.

"And vampires are not all-knowing. He doesn't even know where you live."

"Oh, he knows," Ogden told him. "I feel sure of that. There was something connecting us. He picked up on that. I was different, he said. I would *believe.*"

"And do you?"

He hesitated. Lois brought over the grilled cheese, burned around the edges and a thin wedge of pickle on the side. "Your steak burger will be out in a minute," she said.

"Thank you."

Ogden took a bite, then realized it was impolite to eat before the other person was served.

"Go ahead," Mr. Kowalski offered, but he shook his head no.

"I'm not sure what I believe," Ogden said. "I just wish my sister were not away. This wouldn't be happening if she were here."

"Is your sister some sort of magic talisman?"

"My sister wouldn't let anything bad happen," Ogden said. "She's very strong."

"And you?"

"Here's your steak burger," Lois interjected, thrusting the bloody flesh between them on a plate. "With extra onions. Will there be anything else?"

"No, thank you."

"Me?" Ogden said. "I used to be strong."

He called the Hebrew Home after lunch and told them he had a headache, that he wouldn't be back. He wasn't lying.

"Come with me," Stanley Kowalski said. "My house is just over this way. I want to give you something."

He shouldn't go; he should just head home. Get this crazy notion out of his head. He shouldn't go to a strange man's house. But he followed.

Stanley Kowalski lived in a small, two-family house on Oak Avenue, on the second floor. The road was set two blocks past Ogden's own, off Main; there was a barber shop on the corner, the Friendly Barber Shop. Stanley waved to the barber inside, who was sharpening his razors.

It was a cold day. The wind was whipping, and Ogden's cheeks grew red and hard. He had misplaced his gloves, so he shoved his hands deep down into the pockets of his coat. The sky was a deep, dark gray. Snow beckoned.

The stairs that led to Stanley's apartment were high-polished wood, solid oak, and the smell of the carpeting reminded him of the way the Palace used to smell, on the night of a premiere, back before television when they kept the theater clean for the Friday night crowds. There was a richness to the smell, heady, and it did something to him: the deep scent of an obscure perfume that raised a tickle of memory way back in the unused part of his mind. It was the rush of excitement of going to a premiere at the Palace that he felt, walking up Stanley Kowalski's stairs. For a moment, he forgot all about Samuel Horowitz the vampire, and the fact that Bernie and Chase were a thousand miles away, naked on some sunny beach.

"Here it is," Stanley said, opening his door. "My humble abode."

Inside, the smell was different: dry and dusty, faintly citrusy. A parakeet in a wire cage hung over a frayed soft chair in the living room. It chirped in greeting.

"Hello, Mrs. Tennyson," he said to the bird, moving his face like a crazy man in front of the cage.

Ogden stood in his little foyer, unsure of whether he should proceed much further.

"Ah, Mr. Smith, do not be afraid," he smiled. "Please. Sit down."

"I shouldn't stay," he said.

"But I must give you what we came here for," Stanley said.

Ogden nodded.

Stanley Kowalski disappeared down the hall. Ogden looked around the room, at the newspapers on the floor, the plate full of crumbs and the empty Coke bottle next to the frayed overstuffed chair. Strange how Coke bottles always made him think of a woman: were they meant to? There was a television set, too, but much smaller than Miss Wright's, who'd bought one of the very first models back in 1951. Ogden had never seen one this small. Then he noticed the calendar on the wall: Jayne Mansfield, breasts bared, in a tiny fur-trimmed skirt and boots, shivering atop the hood of a car surrounded by huge drifts of snow.

"Here we are," Mr. Kowalski said, coming down the hall. He had something in his hand. "You take this, Mr. Smith. Wear it around your neck. This will protect you."

It was a crucifix, a large wooden one on a silver chain.

"That will do no good," Ogden protested.

"But why not?"

"He was Jewish," Ogden said plainly.

"Ah," Mr. Kowalski said.

"But *this,*" Ogden said, eyes lighting at the thought as he reached into the pocket of his coat, "this will work." He produced the Star of David. "May I take the chain?"

"But of course. Oh, this is splendid," Stanley said, clapping his hands.

Ogden felt better all ready. Why hadn't he thought of this before?

Mr. Kowalski slid the crucifix off the chain and proceeded to thread it through the small ring at the top of the star. "This was meant to be worn," he said. "May I put it on you?"

"Yes, please," Ogden said, turning his back to him.

Mr. Kowalski slipped the star around Ogden's neck. It dangled awkwardly over his coat.

"There," Stanley Kowalski said, and very quickly he slipped his arms around Ogden, pulling him in, nuzzling his neck.

"Mr. Kowalski!" Ogden shuddered.

"Oh, come, my dear," he soothed, gently biting at his ear lobe. "You came willingly."

"No," he said, but Mr. Kowalski's arms only tightened around him. Ogden couldn't see his face, only hear his words and feel his warm lips pressed against his ear, his neck.

"Foolish boy, to think that vampires can be stopped by silly little trinkets, that they only walk about by night," Stanley Kowalski said, and now his hands, his cold hands, were unbuttoning the front of Ogden's shirt.

"No," he said again, but more meekly this time. "No, please."

Stanley Kowalski moved his cold hands under Ogden's shirt, finding the smooth warmth hidden there.

"Such a dear boy," Stanley said, his lips on Ogden's soft throat. "Such a sweet, innocent child—"

"No," Ogden said dreamily. "Not innocent…"

Mr. Kowalski laughed.

"There was a man—at the school—"

"Hush, hush, dear boy," Mr. Kowalski said. "There shall be no more men. Only me."

And with that, he bit Ogden Smith on the neck.

It had begun to snow.

"It's true," Ogden said, coming out onto the sidewalk, his voice calm and full of wonder as he watched the fragile flakes accumulate on the black wool of his coat. "No two snowflakes *are* exactly the same."

He pulled his coat more tightly around him. It had gotten very cold.

Later, he would not recall the walk home except for the snowflakes. It was as if he walked in a lovely, untroubled dream.

Finally, back at his house, in the last slanting golden rays of the day, he put on a pot of tea and contemplated dinner. "Bernie will want stew," he said out loud. He opened the freezer and looked down into it. No stew meat.

"Oh, dear," he said to himself, and then the sunlight was gone, and the room, he realized, was a hazy shade of blue.

His sweet sense of dreamland faded away.

Bernie's away, Ogden remembered. And it's the third night.

The Star of David still hung around his neck. He clutched it and breathed.

"What should I do?" he said into the darkness, and he pressed his nose up against the windowpane, looking out across the rooftops in the direction of Devil's Hopyard, where he could see, in his mind, the great stone door of the mausoleum in the Jewish cemetery sliding back, and the demons dancing in the hopyard, bowing in strange homage to the returning Samuel Horowitz.... .

The tea kettle was whistling, a piercing sound. Pierced through the heart. He poured some water over his tea bag and inhaled the bitter aroma. "Drink some tea," he told himself.

There it was: the tinny music again, the sound of a Victrola at the Russian Imperial Court, or the sound of an old phonograph spun by old Mr. Wilson, the dean of his school, who would sit there, all night, listening to its seductive sound, who sat there and watched Ogden cry without saying a word or ever moving from his chair. "Don't think your tears will keep you here, you pervert," he said.

There was a knock at the door.

Ogden tensed. He thought for a moment he should hide, but then decided against it. He took another sip of tea and then set the cup down on the table. The knock came again. He took a deep breath and walked over to the door. He spied through the hole.

It was Freddie. The paper boy. He had forgotten.

"Good ev'nin', Mr. Smith," the boy said. His face looked bloated and distorted through the hole.

"Hello, Freddie."

He opened the door and stepped aside to let him enter.

Freddie seemed unsure, but he came inside. He was a tall youth, with long legs and a blond crew cut. He couldn't have been more than thirteen. There was a patch of acne on his chin. He wore a big shiny navy blue coat and a red and white scarf around his neck.

"Now where *is* that envelope my sister left for you?" Ogden mused. His voice was different: lighter, higher.

Freddie shifted his weight from his left foot to his right foot.

Ogden suddenly stopped his search and looked over at the boy, a broad smile on his face. "Freddie, would you like a cup of tea?"

"No, thanks, Mr. Smith. I've got to finish my route."

"It's snowing outside. And so very cold. Are you *sure?*"

"No, thanks. I don't drink tea."

Ogden smiled, approaching him. "Of course not. How silly of me. Boys don't drink tea."

Freddie made an uncomfortable sound.

Ogden touched the boy's cold hard cheeks with each of his fore-fingers. "I could make some hot cocoa," he tempted.

"No, thank you, Mr. Smith."

Ogden watched him for several seconds. Then Ogden's eyes seemed to change, and he looked away. "Here," he said, thrusting the envelope at him. "Go. Get out of here. This place is not safe. He's coming for me. Go. Run. Save yourself."

"Mr. Smith, are you—"

"Go, Freddie! *Run!*" he shouted, and the boy did. Ogden bolted the door behind him.

Heaving, he leaned up against the door. "At least I saved *him,*" he said, his eyes welling up with cold tears.

Ogden clasped his right hand around the Star of David again. He closed his eyes. Now old Samuel Horowitz was dancing in the hop-yard in his floating white burial gown, his thick white hair cascading around him in the darkness. He left no tracks in the newly fall-en snow; no one could trace him. He floated an inch above the snow, sometimes obscured in the swirl of snowflakes, but dancing all the while, a snow dance of death... .

"Stop it," Ogden told himself, sitting down at the kitchen table, pressing his fingers into his temples.

"Bernie will be home tomorrow," he said, trying to convince him-self of something, but what that was remained unclear. "Oh, why did she have to go away and leave me alone now?"

The vampire was closer. He floated over the snow, so white, so pure, so fresh, all the way into town from the hopyard: through the Polish neighborhoods near the river, past St. John the Baptist Church, all the way down Main Street, past the Hebrew Home, past Henry's Diner, past the Palace Theater, up the block toward Ogden's building... .

"Stop it!" he screamed at himself, but then the music got louder, a scratchy old tune, one he knew, but couldn't place, and the scratching was at the window again, and this time it was no squir-rel, it was a hand, an old hand, a very old hand, long gnarled fingers scratching to get in... .

"A vampire must be *invited* into the home."

Ogden Smith backed up into the cupboard in the dark kitchen, staring at the scratch marks in the frost on the window over the sink. "No," he said meekly. "Please don't."

The hand reappeared at the window, scratching away more of the frost.

"You don't want me," Ogden cried. "I'm not what you think. I've been defiled. You don't want me."

But the music only got louder. And when instead of a hand, a face appeared at the window—the face of old Samuel Horowitz, grinning wide and baring his fangs—Ogden screamed with every last vestige of what he once was. He screamed and screamed, but when that was over and no one had come, he finally looked up at the window and said, "Yes. Yes. You might as well come in."

And he tore the Star of David from around his neck, pressing it against his throat for just a moment before tossing it across the kitchen floor, where it clattered and rolled for several seconds, finally settling in the dust beneath the Kelvinator.

Then the window over the sink began to slide open, a screech of icy metal against wood, just as the Trykowskis' great old pendulum clock began to chime the hour, somewhere far off in the building.

"Miss Smith?"

"Yes."

"My name is Stanley Kowalski. No, not Stanley Kowalski."

But Bernie didn't laugh.

The man became serious. "I came inquiring about your brother."

"Are you a friend?"

"I'd only just met him. We had lunch together on Thursday at Henry's Diner."

Bernadette Smith's eyes were still puffy. "And how did he seem to you?"

"Oh, fine, ma'am. Just fine."

"Then you have no clue as to what happened?"

"No, I'm afraid I don't, Miss Smith."

"Then why did you come here?"

"Just to tell you…to tell you what a fine lad your brother was."

Bernadette began to cry. "I should never have left him."

"There, there, my dear," Stanley said, taking the young woman into his arms. He held her in the doorway, stroking her hair.

"He relied on me," Bernadette said into his coat, her words muffled. "And I let him down." She trembled. The man's touch was cold. "Ogden's always been such a sensitive boy. Ever since what happened to him at the school—did he tell you about that?"

"He mentioned something about it."

"Oh, I'll just never forgive myself," Bernie cried.

"Poor dear," Stanley Kowalski said, petting her. "You can't blame yourself. We all wonder if we could have done something."

Bernie looked up at him. "How did you know something had happened?"

The man seemed uneasy for just a moment. "I—I came by in the morning. I saw the ambulance..."

"Oh, please, don't mention it again. Mr. Otfinowski has already described what he found when he came here, just as the sun was coming up, to deliver the milk.... Oh, I should have been here!"

"I'm sorry, dear. I didn't mean to upset you again." Mr. Kowalski's eyes bore down on her. "Might I see him? Perhaps it would do him some good to spend some time with a friend. You will let me see him, won't you?"

"Yes," Bernie said, looking up at him. Her eyes seemed caught by his; she couldn't shake his stare. "Yes. Of course." She turned finally with difficulty and began walking inside the house, leaving the door open for Mr. Kowalski to follow.

"My dear," he called after her graciously. "First you must invite me in."

In his room, Ogden Smith huddled under his blankets, his neck bandaged where Bernie said he had tried to slit his throat with the Star of David. He tried to shield his eyes from the light. He was one of them now. Ogden knew he hadn't tried to slit his throat; the wound was where the vampire had tasted of his blood.

Oh, how the light burned his eyes now. Such would be the way from now on. That much he knew. But for how long? Would old Samuel Horowitz come back for him tonight and kill him? Or would he, instead, make him wait, wait like he had, wait until he was one hundred and six, living only through sheer force of will, always afraid to answer the door, afraid that death would be on the other side, afraid that he would rise up and walk the earth as one of the undead, drinking the blood of the living?

Ogden Smith knew most everything else, but that was the one thing he still didn't know.

Tongues

D. TRAVERS SCOTT

Date: Tue, 2 Jan 1996 17:13:19-0600
To: TomKurtz@teleport.com
From: dioniso@indigo.com (KARL!)
Subject: I'm back!

Hey hon!

Yes, for real, I'm back.

I know you're suspicious, so here's proof: we both fucked that hustler in Merida without condoms. I *know* no one else knows that. So, yes, it's me.

I also know you'll have that damn Powerbook at your side till your breath finale, which I can feel is close but not quite here yet. I can totally see you asking Mr. Reaper to wait a sec while you check your e-mail one last time.

So I want to try to tell you something with this message before you die: I want to let you know where I've been and what's up and all.

BTW, this is totally entre nous. This message will self-erase from your hard drive fifteen minutes after you open it; so there'll be no proof. Nifty trick Father taught me. I'll become a hacker yet!

Anyway, if you tell anyone what I'm about to tell you, they'll just add dementia to your chart in a New York minute.

OK, where the *hell* have I been? Well, that teenage tribal skinhead guy I left you for isn't that young after all.

Here--let me break it to you the way he broke it to me:

Father--that's what I call him. No, it's not some S/M thing--fucked me in mid-air, initiated me into his own Mile High Club, but let me tell you, it's tres less claustrophobic when you're not crammed into some jetliner john.

We were fucking at home on the couch and I was lost, totally out of my body. We could've been going at it for hours--I've told you how I lose time-sense when well-fucked.

Time is sort of fading in relevance these days, though.

So I was lost in the rhythm of Father's cock inside me, hypno-trance metronome of fucking...ocean waves. My eyes were closed...I was worlds away...it was just the best ever, mind-blowing, *really*. Padre was pressed against my back, arms gripped around my chest. His cock was pressed into me--yes, it's bigger than either of ours--and it felt like his mind was pushing its way into mine...his being hijacking mine.

All I was conscious of was his fucking, I didn't even notice the bedsheets slip away, the drapes brush my shoulders.

The cold got me--the gelid night air high above the city. The clammy bath made me open my eyes to see emerald and amber lights drifting by below.

Father had me in his arms, legs wrapped around mine, carrying me through the damp air and fucking me all the while. His grip loosened between thrusts and I felt myself start to drop, then re-secured back into his grasp.

In the cold air, his cum burned inside my ass...mine dropped a hundred feet down onto the city.

When we do it now, I imagine you out in the garden, head raised, mouth open to catch my raining jism.

No, Father is *not* like other boys.

After that night, he asked me to be his Companion.

Here's another postcard:

Father's lying next to me, jerking off furiously with the blood of me. It's a fairly decent lube if you keep it warm and worked up to offset coagulation. What it lacks in viscosity, it makes up for in aesthetic...the shit's beautiful, smeared all over a throbbing dick. When it's thickly covered, it looks like the whole cock's a fresh piece of meat, some swollen internal organ that's been yanked outside of the corpus, twitching with pulse. He shoots and the cum, virginal-white--ha-ha!--flies up into the air like an amoebic angel--but of course it falls.

The white runs down the bloody shaft in stark contrast to the red...I think of the wisps of crimson in my spat-out toothpaste. How I used to worry about those! Gore-Tex floss, baking soda and peroxide anti-tartar toothpaste, sonic plaque-removal tooth-cleaning system, Gly-Oxide peroxide cleansing antiseptic, minty-fresh mouth rinse. All to ward off those dreaded crimson wisps so I could guiltlessly suck cock uncondomed.

I go down on cum and blood now. Father growls and screams from my tongue on his hypersensitive head. The salty cocktail fills my mouth, flavorful liquid flesh. I'm taking him inside me, *swallowing* --oh, Baby, SWALLOWING--ingesting his essence. Cum *and* sangre--how can I describe it? A heavy body, a fleshy substance to it but *unbelievably* smooth. Musky, salty, gamey, yeasty.

My metaphors always sound embarrassingly absurd to Father; he laughs at them: "venison and raw bread dough liquefied in a blender," "a rare roast-beef protein shake."

My persistent need to describe and define these experiences amuses him, endears me to him I think. I'm fresh.

Ultimately, it tastes *more* like dick than dick...as if you were sucking and licking so hard you shoved your tongue inside and sucked that damn thing inside out. As if the skin was no longer a barrier.

We've tried that, you know--per my insistence. Father warned me it didn't work well, but apres I'd heard the anecdote of his first Companion who he'd done it with, I had to try. You know how stubborn I can be. While me-sucking, he bit gently with his lower jaw and slid down rapidly, slicing open the base of my cock with surgical precision. He's so good. His throat constricted around my cockhead but his tongue slithered inside, caressing my tubes and veins, putting pressure on my head from the inside. Erotic catheterization's got *nothing* on this, IMHO!

The warning--which of course I'd ignored--was that even in my new state, I don't heal immediately. No Hollywood insta-morph here...I'm really becoming quite irritated with Hollywood through this whole process. I couldn't get a decent hard-on for a week afterwards. No jacking off, no sex, nothing. Ugh.

The other day I threw on an old denim jacket with a "Live to See the Cure" button on the pocket. Father laughed and said, "You'll see it, all right."

Look, I'm not trying to gloat here.

I'm sorry.

I'm sorry I can't come to you. I can't save you; I'm not a Father and only they can save people. Companeros' blood would just lengthen your suffering. I did ask him, believe me. He said no. I'm sorry. They're actually very selective, very particular about these things. You'd be surprised. They spend years just scouting and studying someone before approaching them to be a Companion. It's not this constant wild hunting, three squares a day. The whole damn planet would be Companions at that rate and they certainly don't want that.

I just want you to know where I went. I did not leave you. I want you to know that. I was not running from you. Maybe I was running to spare myself from your fate. I knew Darren would take good care of you. I think--before all this happened--we knew that. That's why I broke us up, so you could be with him. I knew he'd fall in love with you. He was that type, I could tell, and you *are* quite lovable.

Ironic, though: technically I've beat you to Death--ha-ha, I haven't "beaten you to death" now have I? Close, when you wanted it, but that's different. No, I've died--sort of--before you. Never expected *that*, did we?

I guess the downside is I always thought maybe we'd be together in Death. Yeah, I know, that's rich coming from Senor El Atheisto myself, but lately a lot of my heart's secrets I have 'fessed up to. Soon we'll both be Dead, but not in the same way, so I don't know for sure if we will be any closer or cross paths or what.

No, I did not do all my research before buying. There was no _Consumer Reports_ issue on death and vampirism, OK? I'm still pretty fuzzy on all the details; Father's explanations make zero sense. He said it would start to come together for me circa fifty years from now.

Hell--yeah right--for all I know you're going to become some angel--all those volunteer hours at Outside Inn paying off, I bet-- and come back down here, rip my heart from my chest and chew it up between your pearly whites, swallowing me down into your seraphinic tummy-tum-tum.

Sounds kinda hot, actually.

Sorry--Father said my sense of humor would be one of the first things to blacken.

You were the Love of my Life, you know that, yes? But you're diminishing--you're still the Love of this *most recent* life, but you see, now I'm remembering others. Other lives, loves, languages, countries…. Things are becoming much less linear, the narrative of living is dissolving steadily. My whole focus of grow-achieve-age-die seems irrelevant and artificial now, like Aristotle's chart for dramatic structure or O. Henry's contrived twists. My pasts are becoming more and more present. My future is endless, for all practical purposes. That anxiety, that rushrushrush to accomplish and experience before I testedpositiveseroconverteddied is gone. I can re/live--visit --cycle--play....

Time passes but it's not going anywhere, so why should I care?

Think-you I've chosen a void, an Undead nothingness? Pense a de Wojnarowicz, Haring, Jarmann, Mapplethorpe, Ford, Stern, Eichylberger, Sylvester, Mercury, Callen, Sotomayor, Tumbleston, Esslinger, Rodgers, Barnes, Riggs, Hemphill, d'Allesandro...think of the vacuum of unrealized potential, maturity never reached, never achieved. All the books never written, all the hearts never touched, eyes never opened. Think of the immensity of culture aborted--*that's* a void, *that's* blackness, emptiness, nothingness, death.

Nature abhors a vacuum.

Adios, Love. I won't write again. Here's a farewell kiss to you from all of the many Me's:

El Domini est me shepherd; <<in-the-future>> yo ne desire pas. Il me maketh rester en patures vertes; El me guide <<next-to>> aguas tranquillas.
He restoreth mi soul; El leadeth moi dans les rues de vertu para His nomini's sake.
Girl, though yo traverse thru la vallee de l'ombre de Muerte, <<in-the-future>> je n'ai pas peur de Infernos: para Thou art conmigo; Thy rod y staff <<those-two>> me-console.
Thou work une table <<in-front-of>> me dans le <<general-area-of>> mi ennemis; vos do that oil-head thang; mi cup spilleth a l'excess.
You can bet your ass, simpatico y grace shall me-follow todos los dias de ma vida y je will habite dans le casa d'el Dio ad infinitum.

(Didn't think we could do *that*, huh? Ditto holy water, crucifixes, garlic: all Hollywood melodrama. Sorry to disappoint.

Anyway, it's the words' meanings that are what matters, not who owns them. I love you. Good-bye. Karl.)

Sick Reggie

DAVID NICKLE

"Don't be frightened," Jason whispered, as he opened the door to his kid Reggie's basement room.

"It's not as bad as it looks."

I'm glad, Martin almost said; because from the threshold of the bedroom, little Reggie looked very bad indeed. Skin white like milk, rough like a gravel road where the lesions had healed; bony face and shoulders and hips; hands that trembled; mad little eyes that didn't sit still, didn't really look at anything, either.

Martin wondered what the poor kid was even doing at home and not in the hospital. He wondered, briefly, whether Reggie's long-gone mother had given him the virus; wondered again whether she'd given Jason the same going-away present, and, uncharitably, whether Jason had passed it on again. Whether Martin should be visiting a doctor, making out a will.

It was, he knew, a stupid thing to wonder. Martin had left his wife two years ago—had been monogamous with her for all but the last six months of their nine-year-old marriage, and he had no suspicions that she'd been anything other than faithful to him in their time together. Since then, he'd been scrupulously careful, never gone out without a condom, and nothing he'd done with Jason should have given him any reason to worry.

Still—one look at Reggie, and worry was all he could do.

"Hi, guy," Martin said. Jason was beside him, leaning on the door frame, watching the two of them with obvious anticipation.

Reggie was in his bed, with a reading lamp aimed forward to illuminate his Masked Rider comforter and the spreading pile of Spider Man comic books. A column of machinery that looked like it belonged in a hospital stood in the shadows on the opposite side of his bed, whirring and beeping, distending tubes and ventilators onto a metal stand with many brackets and hooks. The whole room smelled of iodine.

"Say hello to Martin," said Jason. His voice had a strange lilt to it—as though he were talking to a retarded child, or a baby. "Martin's going to stay for awhile. Isn't that right, Martin?"

Reggie looked away, toward the drawn curtain near the ceiling of his basement bedroom. Sunlight painted the thick brown fabric an improbable shade of orange.

"Hi," he said, eyes creeping up across the ceiling. His neck clicked as his head finally turned to look at Martin.

"I'm glad we finally met." Martin stepped into the room, went over to the bed. He sat down on the edge of the mattress, suppressed a shudder, and lied: "I've heard so much about you."

Reggie's eyes went away again, into the shadows behind the machinery. "I'm glad Jason's found someone nice," he said. "Nice for us both."

He smiled, revealing long, crooked teeth, brown with plaque.

Martin smiled back. Reggie wasn't more than twelve years old, but he sounded so—grown up. So precocious. He looked over to Jason.

"Well," said Jason, "it looks as though you two are going to get along—" Jason stopped, and his face fell.

"What—" was all Martin managed to get out, before the comic books rustled and the reading lamp fell over, and Martin felt Reggie's surprisingly sharp teeth sink deep into his arm.

"He doesn't have AIDS, if you're worried about that." Jason wrapped the gauze around Martin's wrist, which was still shaking.

"That's good," said Martin. He had been holding his breath, he realized, and it came out in a long, wavering exhalation. "What does he have?"

"It's not contagious," said Jason. "The condition's congenital—maybe you read about it? Bathory's Syndrome?"

Martin shook his head, grimaced as the gauze moved across the punctures.

"It's rare," said Jason. "Only a few specialists in Canada can even treat the symptoms and—" he stopped then, looked up from his work on Martin's injuries. "Oh Martin, I am so sorry—I should have warned you. Sometimes lately he gets a little weird, a little paranoid—he didn't used to be like this, but the doctors warned me it might—oh, I should have warned you. I am so sorry."

They sat upstairs at the kitchen breakfast-counter. Jason's place was what they used to call open-concept—a long, ranch-style house with huge floor-to-ceiling windows giving a southern view of Lake Ontario through the back garden's trees. The afternoon sun cast a radiant dappling over the waves. Martin shut his eyes against it, swallowed dust.

"As you mention it, why didn't you warn me?"

The kid had missed any major veins or arteries, but there had still been a lot of blood and he had hung on with his teeth, gnawing away at the arm until his chin was streaked red. Martin had fought him, and after a moment Jason came to help, but when Reggie finally let go, Martin was left with the overriding impression it was only because he was ready—because he was *finished,* at least for the time being.

"I'm sorry," said Jason. "It's kind of...kind of a *test* I give to the men I choose."

At that, Martin laughed. It came out sounding choked. "What?" he snapped. "To see if Reggie *likes* them?"

Jason looked hurt. "I didn't expect that to happen," he said. "And no—I'm not testing Reggie. But it's a difficult life with him.... He's very demanding. And I need to see that anyone who comes into the house is up to those demands. Here, hold this down." He put Martin's good hand on the gauze, to hold it in place, then popped open the tin lid on the surgical tape with the end of a pair of scissors. The tape came away with a tearing sound.

"If it's any consolation, Martin," he said, "you passed my test. With flying colors."

Martin opened his mouth to speak, but realized that if he did, he would only say something cruel, sharp. And there was something in Jason's eyes now that blunted any cruelty. Martin looked out the window again, forcing his eyes open, losing his anger in the sunlight.

"Most of the guys I meet," continued Jason, "are way too into themselves. They want a place they can come home to, want the sex, want someone to *love* them. But they got nothing to give; even the ones that seem okay, you know?"

"Sure," said Martin.

"So I show them Reggie. Tell them I've got a kid, but don't warn them or anything...about the way that he is." He put an end of the surgical tape on top of the gauze and pulled it tight around Martin's arm. "And then I just watch them."

"And what do you look for?" asked Martin. "When you're watching them?"

Jason smiled, looked down at his hands then up again, to meet Martin's eyes.

"I look for you," he said, and leaned over from his chair. His mouth tasted salty, and it was warm.

Martin moved his stuff into Jason's that Sunday.

He didn't have much to move—the divorce from Tracy a year ago had left him with very little to call his own; he might have gotten more, but he honestly didn't want to fight her for it. He had been living with two other men in a duplex in Riverdale, spending nights watching Letterman on the communal TV, eating food cooked in the communal microwave and washed down with homemade beer from a brewmaster kit that, strictly speaking, Martin owned a third of.

So when Jason brought the van around, all he had to load up was a couple of boxes of books, his futon and some clothes. Dev offered to help, but Martin shooed him off. His arm was feeling better already, he said, and there wasn't much left to do anyway.

"It doesn't *look* any better," Dev said with mild reproach.

But in the end, he shrugged and wished Martin well. It wasn't particularly sincere—Dev had made it clear that he thought Jason was too old, a little too much of a trim, dashing sugar daddy for Martin's "delicate" state, whatever the hell *that* meant—but Martin took it for what it was worth. Since even before Tracy, he'd decided there was no percentage in burning bridges.

And Dev was at least half-right; Jason was older, and as such he was as trim and dashing as you could hope for, Martin supposed. But Martin could have done without the sugar-daddy moniker. Dev and the others, he reminded himself, didn't know about Reggie—didn't know about the sacrifices that Jason made every day, caring for his ill son.

"Who's looking after Reggie?" asked Martin later, as they inched their way through the busy Beaches streets toward Jason's place.

"Nadia," said Jason. "She's a nurse with the institute—comes by three times a week as a rule, and they have her on call for when I have to be away."

Martin briefly wondered what institute Jason was talking about. But the question wouldn't come, and what he said was, "That must be expensive."

Jason shrugged. "It's covered," he said, flicking the turn indicator as they approached the entrance to his street. The pavement dropped off sharply as the road sloped down through a tunnel of leaves and needles, to the lakefront houses. As they rounded the last bend, Martin could see the car in Jason's driveway—in *their* driveway, he corrected. It was an old Tercel hatchback, and its rear seats had been collapsed to hold a stack of boxes and cases that reached nearly as high as the roof. He didn't recognize the company name—Vita-Derm—but they reminded him of some of the Amway products, hair spray and nail polish and skin cream, a neighbor had tried to foist onto Tracy when they were together.

"Nadia's car?" he asked, and Jason nodded.

"Don't worry," he said. "She won't stay."

As Jason pulled the van up behind it, Martin was sure he saw someone stirring in the passenger seat. But as it turned out, the seat was empty. Nadia had come alone. And she was after all in the basement, tending to Jason's sick boy—

No, that was wrong.

She was tending to *their* sick boy, looking after *their* Reggie. Martin would have to start thinking that way, if he were going to make this arrangement work.

Martin grabbed a box from the back of the van while Jason went to open the front door. A shot of pain went up his arm—the box was full of books, and it was heavy—but as he shifted position, the pain dulled.

By the time he crossed the threshold, his arm felt fine. He set the box down by the hall closet, and went back outside to finish the van.

It wasn't until the third trip that Martin realized Jason had gone downstairs. He stood alone in the house's wide main room. Outside, thick gray clouds and a strong east wind painted the lake water the color of clay.

Our boy, Martin said to himself. *Our* Reggie.

I should be there too.

And so he left the van outside, and crossed Jason's wide main floor to the basement stairway.

They hadn't wanted children. Tracy had made that clear at the outset, and Martin hadn't felt strongly enough about it one way or another to put up any argument. Based on the dreary existences of his ex-wife's friends and siblings who'd gone the parenting route, he could understand where her arguments came from. Kids lock you in your house; suck the life out of your conversation, your interests; trammel your dreams and drain your bank account. They make you old before your time.

In the end, however, their agreement on the issue turned around. In the days after he came out, Tracy wondered aloud if he had acquiesced so easily, not because he hadn't wanted a baby, but because he hadn't wanted her. His agreeability had retroactively become a kind of abuse, a backhanded rejection.

Martin had told her the interpretation was superficial, and unnecessarily vindictive. At the time, he saw his sexuality as a newborn itself—before he had discovered it, his life and the decisions he'd made were untainted by these new desires, because they simply had not existed. Not, he had naïvely assumed, until he had willed them to.

Since that time, Martin had come to realize he'd been lying to himself about his feelings—they had been with him always, a constant desire not even half-buried in denial. But he had remained certain that his feelings about children and parenting were separate from that—and consistently ambivalent.

Today, though, he wasn't as certain.

By the time he'd reached the bottom of the stairs, it was as though he were being tugged—as though some new instinct, a decidedly paternal one, were suddenly revealed. A line through his life that had been drawn tight.

Jason stood outside the bedroom, arms crossed. Inside, Martin could hear the high whir of an electric motor, mingled with a slurping—the vacuum-cleaner suck of pus from a wound.

"I can never watch," he said, unfolding his arms.

Martin shuddered. "I bet," he said, and sat down on the old sofa by the bar. "What's going on in there, anyway? Dare I ask."

Before Jason could answer, Reggie interjected, from behind the door: "Hey! Is that Martin?"

A low woman's voice—Nadia's, no doubt—muttered something unintelligible, stern.

"No way!" Reggie sounded improbably healthy, energetic—Martin had a hard time matching the voice with the sick, sophisticated little boy he'd met earlier in the week. "I want to see my friend Martin!"

Martin caught Jason looking at him, and grinned, lowered his eyes. "I guess I pass," he said.

"Pass?"

"Reggie's test," said Martin, and flexed his bandaged hand. "His taste test."

Jason came over and sat down at the other end of the couch. Martin started to get up, but Jason put his hand on his arm, gently pulled him back down.

"We'd better wait," he said, "until Nadia's done."

The nurse was thin, with cheekbones that would have been appropriate on a fashion model if height were the sole criterion. But as she stepped around the door, the light from behind her made shadows above them, hollowed her eye sockets beneath an equally prominent brow. Nadia from the institute was getting on, Martin thought, egged forward by a strange prickle of dislike in his belly. She must be pushing forty now, maybe older.

And her peasant stock is beginning to show.

The voice in Martin's head was a creaking, old leather strap pulled tight.

"Mr. Edmunds." She looked right past Martin, talking to Jason. "We shouldn't disturb him now—Reggie is sleeping."

She set down a big brushed-steel suitcase by the radiator, and pulled a clipboard from under her arm—there was the Vita-Derm logo again, Martin saw, stenciled on the back.

"Doctor Lerner wants to come by personally in two weeks. In the meantime, here is something—" She opened the clipboard, and pulled off what was unmistakably a check, "—to keep you going."

Jason stood, took the paper from her, and pushed it into his breast pocket. "Thanks," he said. "Oh Nadia, you haven't met—"

"Martin?" For the first time, Nadia looked directly at Martin. Her lips pulled up into a little smile, and she extended her hand. "Reggie's new friend." Her hand was warm—it felt almost feverish in Martin's grip. "And Mr. Edmunds' new—what?" Her smile didn't change. Martin didn't know what to say.

"Well," said Jason, breaking what was turning into an awkward silence, "let's go upstairs. Martin's moving his stuff in today, and we should get back to it."

"Then I'll let you," said Nadia, and released Martin's hand. She turned away, and as she hefted the suitcase, Martin was sure he could hear the sound of liquid sloshing inside. She turned to Martin as she climbed.

"You should look after that wrist," she said.

Peasant, said the leather voice again in Martin's skull. He resisted the urge to rub under the bandage, and followed Jason and Nadia up the stairs into the gray afternoon light. They were talking quietly, with a certain intensity. But try as he might, Martin couldn't make out a word of what they were saying.

They went to bed early after ordering in some chicken wings and polishing off a six-pack of Corona. Martin looked in on Reggie three times throughout the evening—just to say hi, Martin explained; didn't want the poor kid to think he was ignoring him— but Reggie slept soundly in the dark of his bedroom, snoring quietly underneath the blinking red and green lights of the apparatus. Martin wasn't about to disturb him.

"I'm glad you're here with me," said Jason. The bed was actually in a loft room, and rainwater made a pattern of rivulets on the skylight that the city-glow cast onto their bare flesh—a great, writhing tattoo from the clouds. Martin laughed at the image, ran his finger along the inside of Jason's thigh.

"Glad to be here," he said, and made a fist around Jason's cock. His new lover's back arched as he drew the flesh forward along the shaft—coaxing it harder—relaxed his grip then pulled again.

Like milking a cow, isn't it? came the voice.

Martin shook his head, blinked. He opened his hand and shifted so he touched Jason with his fingertips at the stem, his wrist brushing the tip. He felt very cold suddenly, so he pushed himself up against Jason's flank. Jason obligingly shifted, and Martin fell into the crack of his ass. At the back of his mind, he thought about getting a condom. That was what he always did, after all—he never went in without protection.

Martin might have withdrawn then, gone to find one in his luggage. But he froze in place, his back rigid—listening to the voice.

Just like milking a cow. It carried a sing-song taunt to it now. *Martin the milkmaid.*

Martin let go, rested his fingers in the thick hair of Jason's lower belly. His cock felt limp in Jason's cool ass.

Jason blinked, propped his head on a pillow.

"Well don't stop now," he whispered.

Come see me, said the voice—no longer leather-dry.

"Sorry," said Martin, and took Jason's cock again. "Just got distracted."

Come see me tonight, said Reggie in his head.

Martin helped Jason finish, but both could tell his heart wasn't in it. And the lassitude seemed contagious; when Jason finally came, Martin could barely tell.

Jason drifted off to sleep after only a perfunctory offer to return the favor, and as his snores became more regular, Martin rolled out of bed. He slipped into Jason's old bathrobe and padded into the hall.

Martin wasn't going to ask Reggie how it was that *his* voice had crept into his thoughts since he had arrived here. But he didn't feel that it was his place to disobey that voice, either.

The main-floor living room was awash in unfamiliar shadows from the picture windows, where the lake light caught and transformed tree branches, like the water on the skylight. Martin crossed it to the basement stairs.

"I'm coming," he murmured, then added, for reasons he couldn't quite grasp:

"Don't be angry."

"Nadia thinks you're a hustler," said Reggie. He was sitting propped up in his bed—no comic books this time, and his comforter was pulled up over his chest, making his head appear disembodied. His eyes were different too, steadier in the dim light from the basement rec room. "She thinks you've come here to take Jason for all he's worth."

"I don't think she knows me." Martin touched his hand to the wall switch in Reggie's room, hesitated over it.

"It's all right," said Reggie. "You can turn on the light in here."

Martin flipped the switch, and squinted as the room brightened.

"If you're not a hustler, then what are you?" Reggie's face twisted into a parody of a grin. "My new *daddy?* My *mommy?* Or—" something under the covers rustled then, "—a milkmaid?"

Martin felt his knees tremble at that—it was the same phrase that had entered his mind upstairs, in bed. *Martin the milkmaid.* And from the way the kid was looking at him as he said it, Martin could tell he knew it. Under the bandage, the wound on his wrist went numb, and Reggie's grin widened.

"I'm a hustler," said Reggie. His teeth were very long, and Martin could see the tip of his tongue—fat and pale and somehow larval—as it caressed their edges. "But it looks like I've been hustled myself. By my old *chum* Jason. And God-damned Bathory."

Martin thought again about what Jason had said about his kid's paranoia—and if he tried, he could almost put down his unease with it. *Reggie's just a sick little boy, and sometimes he gets delusional in the night. Don't let it faze you.*

Martin could almost do it—except for the voice.

Why didn't you go get a tetanus shot? it asked him, soft now in the back of his brain.

"What?"

Reggie repeated, aloud: "Why didn't you get a tetanus shot, after I bit you? Or at least go to a doctor?"

Martin sat down at the foot of Reggie's bed. A leg pushed up the blankets into a sharp tent, too close. "How...how do you know I didn't?" Martin asked.

The leg moved closer, nudged Martin's ass. It felt like being jabbed with a stick.

"You didn't go to the doctor because I didn't want you to. I have some things to say to you and I wanted to make sure you would listen. And you don't need a tetanus shot, because people don't get tetanus from my kind."

Reggie laughed, a cold whisper of lake wind through dead wood. "Your...kind?"

"I'm glad you came down tonight," said Reggie. There was a rustle of movement, and the comforter fell away from his chest. The skin there was mottled white and yellow, pulled tight across prominent ribs. Wires from the machinery were taped along his chest. A transparent plastic tube snaked down his arm and disappeared under the comforter. It was pink with blood.

"I'm in a lot of trouble here, Martin. These bastards are sucking me dry. Me!" Reggie's black little eyes held Martin's—he couldn't look away, couldn't deny them. "I need your help."

Martin felt his eyes being drawn now away from Reggie's, towards the machinery. He leaned closer, following the tube from Reggie's arm down the side of the bed, and into an institutional-green metal box. There were dials on it, but Martin couldn't read what they said—they were labeled in neat Cyrillic script.

He didn't have any trouble figuring out what the thing was used for, though. A second tube came out of it, leading to a tall plastic bottle, in a rack behind the machinery tower. That tube was also pink, and blood dripped steadily from the end of it, into a growing reservoir at the bottom of the bottle.

Oh, it was easy to see what the thing was for. It was a regulator, a pump. A milking machine, for Reggie's blood.

"They're sucking you dry," said Martin. "Jesus, what—"

What do they need your blood for? he meant to ask.

But the question didn't finish.

Milkmaid, said Reggie. *Here.*

Reggie asked Martin to undo the bandages on his wrist, and Martin didn't hesitate to obey. The bandages fell away, and Reggie took the hand, lined up the old wounds with his teeth. Of its own will, or so it seemed, Martin's free hand reached over to the IV tube and squeezed it shut, pulled it from the stopper. Touched it to his tongue.

And the blood flowed delicately through them both, in a long, conjoining string.

Martin called in sick at the bookstore the next day. He would have liked to have confronted Jason about the things he'd seen the night before, talked over the unsettling dreams that had followed him even into the daylight.

But Jason was gone when he woke up. There was a note on the refrigerator: *Look after Reggie. Be back tonight.* Underneath was a telephone number for *Nadia,* at the *Institute.* It was pretty presumptuous—at any other time, Martin would have torn a strip off Jason for taking off like that, leaving Martin holding the bag for *his* kid. Didn't Martin still have a life of his own, for Christ's sake?

Martin was in no shape to go anywhere today, though. Somehow, he had found his way back up to bed in the night, and when he awoke, he clutched at the comforter, stealing its warmth. His wrist was no longer bandaged, but wrapped in a towel, and everything below it felt cold, like hamburger—Martin couldn't bring himself to look. He wanted to puke, but couldn't, quite. Something tasted awful in his mouth, something that wouldn't go away even after he'd brushed his teeth and gargled.

And the dreams... .

There were other questions he had for Jason than just why, on the first Monday of their cohabitation, he'd left Martin alone to look after his sick little kid.

After the past night, after the events and after the dreams, Martin wasn't even sure that Reggie *was* Jason's kid.

Martin sat in the kitchen for what seemed like hours, trying to put the dreams together, make them parse with the blood machine and the voice, the cooling meat at the end of his wrist.

He remembered a gravel pit under the moon. Two boys, running through the night—one fast, supple-limbed, leading the way; the other a little frightened, slowed by his own heaviness, his pubescent awkwardness, but pulled on by a desire that Martin recognized instantly. The boy ahead was beautiful—flesh like a girl's, pale and smooth, drawn tight over a sleek young frame; sweat glistening like beads of mercury in the moonlight; thick-lashed eyes, whose depths contained an invitation that was at once irresistible, and dangerous.

The boy behind only wanted a touch.

And the dream shifted, and the two boys were at the top of a mound of dirt, crouched in some scrub grass and rock. Martin remembered feeling the breeze, warm and moist, and thinking—*It's midsummer in 1963, and even the nights are hot.* The fat boy was breathing heavily, his heart was thundering—both from the exertion of the climb and the proximity to the other.

"Go ahead," said that other, his face a shadow in the moonlight. Only his eyes shone through—as if with a light of their own.

"You know you want to. *Faggot.*"

The words brought out complicated feelings in the fat boy. Twelve years old, and nobody likes being called *faggot.* The fat boy was pretty sure he wasn't a faggot anyway—it was just a feeling, and it would go away soon enough, maybe in high school when he met some okay-looking girls. He wasn't a fag, or a queer, or anything else.

But there was also an invitation in those words. And the look in the eyes was unmistakable.

"O-okay." The fat boy reached out, and the other took his hand.

"You're shaking like a leaf," he said, and opened his mouth. Moonlight gleamed off long, sharp teeth.

That was all that Martin could recall of the gravel pit, but there were other scenes. The fat boy at home, with a broken arm. He had fallen in the gravel pit, fractured the bone up near the shoulder, and

the doctors had put a cast on that would have kept him at home
even if his mother hadn't grounded him. Even after a phone call to
his friend's aging parents, who she admitted seemed like good, solid
people, she had forbidden him from spending any time with the
other. "He's a bad influence," she'd said. "And that's final."

Which was why he was so surprised when two nights after, the
other showed up at his bedroom door. He wore a pair of blue jeans
and a denim jacket that was faded nearly to white.

"My mom says I'm not supposed to see you."

"It doesn't matter."

"How'd she let you in?"

"She didn't."

"You bit me and you pushed me off the hill. Why did you do that
to me?"

"Because you're a queer. I didn't want your fucking fag queer
cooties all over me."

"I'm not a queer."

"You're a faggot, Jason." He smiled. "And you're mine now, faggot."

The fat boy—Jason—*Jason* felt like crying, but he didn't let himself.

"I'm not a faggot," he said, trembling now with rage. "And I'm
not yours. My mom *says.*"

The other laughed at that, and this time the sound was unmistakable—it was sick little Reggie's laugh, as dry and old and dead
then as it had been last night. Preserved across the decades, laughter
in amber.

At around noon, Martin found the courage to unwrap the towel
and examine his wrist. It didn't look nearly as bad as it felt; just two
neat little puncture marks, the flesh puckered white around them.
There wasn't even much blood on the towel—no more than specks,
the size that a shaving cut might leave. Reggie had been more careful drinking his blood this second time.

Martin went to the medicine cabinet, got out a roll of fresh gauze
and rebandaged the wound. Then he went down to the basement,
and took a look in Reggie's room. He was sleeping soundly—not
even a snore—and once again, Martin was unsurprised.

After all, Martin had read his Anne Rice. He went to see the
Coppola film when it came out a couple of years ago, and he just
about grew up with the Hammer films. All of them agreed—during

the day, vampires preferred to sleep. He'd seen Reggie awake in the daylight hours, but as Martin thought about it, he hadn't seemed as intelligent, as *strong* as he had in the night.

Hell, Reggie'd barely been able to speak over Martin's own thoughts yesterday afternoon. But through the night, he'd been strong enough to send a dream that explained as coherently as anything could, the particular origins of Reggie's relationship with his "father" Jason.

As he walked alone through the empty house, other sendings fell into place in Martin's mind—seemingly disparate images that took their time to come together as a comprehensible story. It was a story, Martin came to realize, of the vampire's life.

Dates were difficult to tell—it might have been any time in the past half-century that the vampire was made. The making itself transpired in some Eastern European village—he remembered thatched roofs and candlelight; but it was a pike, or a halberd, some antique pole-arm, that killed the vampire who'd turned Reggie. The metal of its newly forged blade gleamed in the torchlight as Reggie watched on, the older vampire's eon-tainted blood still wet on his chin, already working its changes.

From that night on, Reggie didn't mark calendars well—and he stayed away from the places where history left its more recognizable scars, so Martin couldn't mark the time well, either. Years passed in thick wilderness, hunting down peasants and travelers on the desolate roads and passes of a younger world, huddling in caves and pits against the searing daylight. Running and leaping under the moon.

The vampire Reggie spent some years in what was unmistakably Russia—a wandering child between villages, past churches topped with onion domes and packed with pre-Revolutionary despair. It was in Russia, Martin thought, that Reggie developed a taste for towns, the life of a child.

He hooked up with a family of Jews at some point shortly thereafter—traveled with them to Poland. Stayed with them in his thrall until too many years accumulated, and neighbors began to wonder too loudly about the eternal child and his aging parents. Then there was a Czech family, and after them, a German couple—more Jews, childless then, young and hopeful about the future—and these he had the foresight to push to Canada.

There were few persistent themes in the little vampire's life. One of those few was a Romanian noblewoman—Contessa Elizabeth Bathory. The same name, Martin noted, as that of the syndrome from which Reggie supposedly suffered.

At least four times, he managed to escape from this woman's agents: once in a cave, on the edge of a mountain pass; in Russia; in Prague, and again in Berlin. They never tried to kill him, nothing nearly so melodramatic. But they wanted him. *She* wanted him.

Martin started to make notes on a scratch pad that Jason kept by the phone, then stopped again.

As it all coalesced, he was no longer certain that the contents of his dreams—and indeed the events of the night before—were things he felt comfortable having Jason know about.

He thought again about the pump beside Reggie's bed—a pump for blood transfusions, its flow reversed, so that it drained the vampire every night. Kept him weak. He thought about the Contessa, and the institute, Vita-Derm. And Nadia, who came in from time to time to adjust that pump, collect the blood, and who just yesterday afternoon told Reggie she thought that *Martin* was the hustler.

Martin lifted the pen that he had been using to make notes, and tapped it against the counter. As his own, newly infected blood tickled through his veins, he let himself travel back again through Reggie's myriad childhoods. It was incredible, he reflected, what a small yet significant piece of them the vampire's captivity here truly was.

A big, four-masted schooner was cutting west across the water, towards the harbor, and the early evening sun made its sails into fulsome, luminescent things.

Martin put the telephone back in its cradle and walked over to the windows, drew the blinds across the view.

Jason had never tried to fuck Reggie, although for many years he had wanted to. Jason had gone to high school, to university, on from there to work, always with Reggie in tow. At first, Reggie was his baby brother; if anyone asked, the two of them were orphans, and now all they had in the world was each other. The story was very sad, and pretty much true—Reggie had taken care of his own aging parents first, and then, when Jason proved too squeamish to do the job himself, he'd brought down Mr. and Mrs. Edmunds as well. And the two sad little orphans were brothers as well—although not in the way most people assumed.

Sick Reggie

By the time he'd finished university, Jason had pretty much gotten over his prepubescent lusts—he was no pedophile, after all, and Reggie was forever a boy of twelve. But as he grew older, the lines on his face multiplying and the fat in his middle swelling, Jason came to realize he wanted something else from Reggie. Something more...permanent.

"I'd let you fuck me first," Reggie had told him the first night he broached the subject. "And *that's* not going to happen."

Jason begged and wheedled and promised. He even made threats, weak and hollow things, took them back and reasserted them again as the argument swayed. But Reggie was firm—he would not share his own blood, turn Jason into a thing like himself. He hadn't bestowed that gift in the past, not to a single generation of the parents he'd enthralled in his lifetime, and he certainly wasn't about to now— *"not to this grizzled old queer."*

At some point during this period of their lives together, Jason met a man from the Bathory Institute. Reggie was not privy to the discussions—the institute man gave Jason a drug that clouded his mind, and kept his scheming a secret—so Reggie had assumed it was only another of Jason's sad little affairs.

Martin staggered back into the living room, managed to find an armchair to keep himself from falling as the memory of the institute's first visit came to him. It was a vivid, steel spike through optic nerve—as jumbled and incomprehensible as it had been to Reggie.

Darkness as a welcome shadow, protecting against the light; then a brilliance, as the intersecting wood is yanked free, and Reggie thinks: Hunters, churchmen with stakes and hammers, crucifixes and holy water, bushels of garlic—where is Jason? *And Jason is there, indistinct in the light, looking away as the man from the institute leans forward, hypodermic in hand. And then a prick through flesh, and the needle squirts fire under the vampire's skin.*

"Now you're free," says the institute man. "We've got him where he can't hurt you. He's down."

Still, Jason doesn't look. "I'm sorry, Reggie. I won't let them take you away. I'm sorry."

Even over the years—even to Martin—Jason's apology was a smug and hateful thing. In the face of it, Reggie probably would have killed him then, had the fiery serum in his veins not made him too weak for it. But he wasn't too weak to scream, and that is what he did—again and again until—

Martin stopped it, forcing his own eyes open onto the still-painful afternoon light. He shouldn't be letting this vampire mind-trick pull him too far in, he knew. That was how they got you in the stories—suckered you in with false pathos, mimicked the voice of a loved one, or just mesmerized you with the confidence of their ancient gazes.

Hell, Martin told himself. *Reggie's already gotten me to call—*

He stopped again, thought about it, looked over at the telephone. From outside, he could hear the low chugging sound of a small car engine pulling into the driveway.

Jesus.

Reggie'd gotten him to call the number on the fridge; Nadia at the institute. What had he *said* to her?

Martin couldn't remember. But it must have been convincing.

A car door opened and slammed, and scarcely an instant later, a staccato knocking came at the door. Martin felt his shoulders tremble—not in fear as much as weakness. As hunger.

"Did you call 911?" Nadia snapped as he entered, and when he said no, she nodded with satisfaction. "Good. Better I deal with this myself—hospital would misdiagnose. You didn't sound good on the phone. Are you all right?" She had set down the big metal briefcase near the top of the stairs, turned to Martin, and raised her eyebrows in question, all as she spoke.

"Fine," said Martin, fumbling to pull the front door shut against the light. "Not bad. I...slept badly," he finally added, weakly.

"Ah." She looked at the living room, the drawn curtains. "Where is Mr. Edmunds?"

"He went out this morning." Martin swallowed, his throat hurting in the process. "Said he'd be back tonight."

"Well," she said, looking back at him with an unreadable expression. "It's a good thing that you were here to call me, then. Who knows what might have become of poor little Reggie if you hadn't been so...quick thinking."

Another image came into Martin's head, then—not sent by Reggie, not another picture from another life—but a vision here, a transformation of the now. In the whiteness of Nurse Nadia's flesh.

It had become skinned fish, raw prawn in a Chinatown market bin—broken by subcutaneous veins and capillaries that blurred and resolved again as the flesh thickened and bunched over top. There was evidence of bone in the shape, but nothing solid seemed to move within the gelatinous folds. Nothing but liquid, sea-cold viscera—as pale and terrible as Reggie had been, when Martin first saw him a few days ago.

And then, the voice again:

This is how they are.

Nadia seemed unaware of the transformation, if that's what it was. She lifted her suitcase, and turned down the stairs even as Martin turned away from the sight of her. The voice in his head devolved into laughter.

The taste in his mouth from that morning resolved itself then, and the idea that Martin had been avoiding all day became inescapable.

He was tasting blood. Sweet, musty, and indescribably *ancient* blood. Pulled by a pump, from the vampire's veins. Sucked from a bottle before sleep, in Reggie's basement room.

This is how they are.

This, Martin realized, was how *he* had been. Until Reggie had made him, last night.

Martin started after the wet thing that had been Nadia.

Stay there, said Reggie in his mind, laughter gone and replaced by hunger, slyness. *The peasant is mine.*

Martin found he couldn't disobey. Dimly, he remembered the other rule from vampire stories, about the hierarchies that came when one of the undead turned another. A new thing had been born in him today, and this thing was more a part of Reggie than it was himself... .

And it was powerful. God, if Jason had known how powerful, would he have still wanted it so? Or would he have wanted it more?

He was interrupted by a shriek from downstairs. The fact of it didn't surprise him—he had more than an inkling of the trap that he'd helped Reggie lay, the revenge he had in mind—but the tone of it did. There was no terror in Nadia's voice—it was enraged, an adrenal shout that superseded everything else. There was a tumbling sound, followed by a crash, and more shouting—

—and Martin was moving. It seemed like his feet didn't even touch the floor as he crossed it to the basement stairs, and again he was airborne as he descended them. He was nearly blinded with pain brought on by the other shriek, this one in his skull. But he couldn't stop moving, any less than he could have moved a moment ago, when Reggie's needs had been opposite.

The door to Reggie's room was open, and bedding curled out from its base, like the cooling entrails of some great beast. The light weaved and bobbed through the open door, casting a moving rectangle of yellow over the contours of the bar, the couch.

Martin flew into the light, and there he joined the struggle against the white thing Nadia. It was threatening his beautiful, healthy boy Reggie, puckered white lips round over snarling mouth, metal things flashing in the curls of its fingers. Martin could not permit it, and he dove at the creature's back, even as she howled and turned to face him.

And everything is new. Martin has changed utterly in these moments, the vampire blood moving from his belly to his limbs, remaking him at the level of cells. He sees how it has been for Reggie now, no need to imagine, no need to extrapolate back and forth. Time is amber, all experience is coalesced into a single continuum—a string, drawing him forward, showing his path behind. Thread through Minos' maze.

The nurse is beneath him. She has half-turned; there is the metal in her hand, a pin that gleams a little red in the light. No matter— she is too slow, too low and white and soft to be a threat. He grasps her face between his hands, lets his jaw unhinge. His fingers dig beneath her flesh as if it were gelatin, and in a moment, his teeth burrow there, too. He tastes with bone, as he draws her in through blood-forged pathways inside his incisors.

Reggie craves revenge—that is why he made him: to summon her here, to exact his revenge for decades of indignity. In the face of Reggie's weakness, Martin has become the instrument of that revenge. His new purpose hums along his nerves, canceling thought, erasing emotion.

And that is when the metal touches his chest.

What happened next is barely recollection; Martin's memories and understanding of Reggie's life are better than his understanding of that moment in the basement. He remembers how the metal dug into his chest, remembers the shot of dulling fire that sped through him then. He clawed at the thing, sucked deep through his teeth, pummeled at bone and viscera. But the fire was there, too, and it robbed him of his strength as fast as he could retain it. And then came insensibility, and silence.

"Martin."

He hears this voice as a buzzing in his ear, insect sound in the brilliant fire of the dying day.

"I'm sorry, Martin."

It is Jason. Martin opens his eyes as he recognizes the voice, and looks up at the white, lumpen shape that hangs over him. The light is painful to his eyes, to his flesh, but Martin makes himself look. This is Jason. This is his lover. White thing, dead-alive. Adam's apple, up and down long mottled throat, nervous and slippery. Jason couldn't look at Reggie years ago, and tonight he cannot meet Martin's eyes any better.

Martin tries to move but realizes that he has been well-restrained with thick leather straps, on some kind of a stretcher. Other figures slide through the air around him—he recognizes the thing that was Nadia, but there are more, thick-waisted eels whose voices buzz in unguessable tongues.

"You said he would be all right, that he hadn't been bitten," says Nadia, and Jason turned fully away from him to answer her.

"I didn't want to lose him—"

"—and that's what you've done," she finishes. "Lost him. You are so stupid. So young, even as you age."

"That's the idea, isn't it?" Jason is trying quip, but his voice betrays him. "Look, I couldn't know Reggie'd let him drink his blood. Couldn't—"

"I don't know why they let you stay with Reggie," she snaps. "You're a fuck-up from word go."

Now Jason's fear bubbles to the surface. "That was the deal, Nadia—you get the blood, I get Reggie. You can't go back on the deal."

"You almost got me killed, you shit," she says. "Don't talk to me about deals."

And then the stretcher moves under him, and Jason and Nadia pull into the past—into his history. Martin is about to scream when the light is cut off, and he is comfortably enshrouded in the shadow of a great, black van. From somewhere in that shadow, he hears another sound, a bubbling sigh that speaks of an ancient weariness, a bone-deep defeat.

Reggie? he asks with his mind. But there is no answer now. Martin tries to move his mouth to make the word aloud—but he has forgotten how. It comes out as a sick dog sound.

Below him, an engine roars alive, and the shadows move away from Jason's house. Martin, bound and silent, moves with them.

There is a place in the woods north of there, bounded by high fences and patrolled by hard men with dogs and rifles, where the Bathory Institute and the Vita-Derm Corporation have sunk a foundation into the earth. It has many chambers, this foundation, and goes down three full stories into the coolness of the soil. Even the highest floor is covered against the light. So those who inhabit it do not scream much.

It is not a place for studying disease. The chambers are filled with advanced medical machinery, it is true—and the specialists are better trained than most physicians. But there is no study; there is no treatment here. The specialists at the Bathory Institute know everything they need to know of Bathory's Syndrome. They have studied the teachings of the Contessa well—some of them have studied with the Contessa, and they know what just a drop of the hemoglobin from their patients can achieve, if it is blended just so, applied in cream or bath oil. They know what price it can fetch.

What price eternal youth? To walk the world day and night, day and night, and again and again and so, without ever feeling the hunger and ever fearing the sun? Not too dear a price, not for the Vita-Derm agents and their customers, here in the depths of the Bathory Institute.

Those who inhabit the institute do not scream much. The I.V. is attached at their collarbones, driven in past long-dead nerves, and the pump pulls just so—the blood leaves them with a soothing thrum, not too much, not too little. They do not struggle.

Martin inhabits a niche all his own here; he does not know if Reggie is here too; the drugs they have given him make him deaf to Reggie's call. But he thinks Reggie is gone, now; he remembers the deal that Jason mentioned, and thinks that he would have called the institute on it by now.

As his lungs labor and his hemoglobin multiplies and drains, he sometimes dreams that Reggie has not been taken back to Jason's bright house on the lake but has indeed escaped; maybe he turned one of the white things here, maybe he finally found the strength to do it all himself. Thin yellow lips pull back from crooked, sharp teeth as the blood-pump hums through the eons-long night.

Beautiful young Reggie, flesh smooth as a girl's, gossamer hair tickled by wind from the sea, moonlight reflected in a sheen of mercurous sweat.

Sick little Reggie, reborn into the night.

Retribution for Golgotha

WICKIE STAMPS

> *And when Pilate saw that he was accomplish-*
> *ing nothing, but rather that a riot was starting,*
> *he took water and washed his hands in front of*
> *the multitude, saying, "I am innocent of this*
> *Man's blood; see to that yourselves."*
> *And the people answered and said, "His blood*
> *be on us and on our children."*

Matthew 27:24-25

Dismas stood up, walked over to the bar and reached for a bottle of Wild Turkey.

"Any there for me?" A long, lean arm slipped under Dismas' arm and grabbed the half-full bourbon bottle. Dismas knew it was Simon. As Dismas turned and handed a guest a drink, he glanced at Simon who was, as always, magnificently poised. His long, pale fingers were wrapped around the bourbon bottle and he was leaning back against the sideboard, sipping his drink. His shirt slightly open, Simon was temptation in the flesh. He knew his work and performed it well.

Dismas walked over to the young man seated on the couch, sat down and continued their inane conversation. As always, the research on the young man was thorough. Relying heavily on the Mormons' extensive genealogical records, Dismas knew that this particular young man was a descendent of Golgotha, where Jesus was crucified. Unlike the other young men who were descendants of the multitude, this one's lineage led directly to the priests and elders of Golgotha, the ones who had orchestrated Jesus' crucifixion. Dismas, whose hand now rested on the boy's shoulder, smiled to himself at the irony of using the Mormons to track the Golgothan descendants. But the Mormons, obsessed with lineage, never erred.

As Dismas continued his seduction, he thought about Golgotha. He knew it well. Golgotha was where he too had been crucified. Dismas was one of the two thieves. He offered the young man a cigarette and stared at Simon. Pushed by the multitude into Jesus' path, Simon.

Dismas casually lowered his hand onto the young man's thigh and continued his seduction.

Simon circulated about the room, leaned against a wall and admired Dismas' progress. Clearly the boy was his. It was common practice for Simon to stand in the shadows and watch Dismas manipulate his prey. Sometimes, usually when they were in the bars tracking a descendant, Simon even joined Dismas, each taking turns sucking their victim's cock. Or better yet, entering dark alleys, pulling down the young men's pants and shoving their cocks deep into the asses of their prey, the impending fate of their unwitting victims sweetening their pleasure.

After a final look at Dismas, Simon exited the room and walked slowly down the hall. As he proceeded, he thought about Dismas and the day of their first meeting. Simon had followed the crowds up to the sight of the crucifixion. All around Simon, men had cursed and spat on Jesus as well as Dismas. The women had torn at their clothes and hair, despairing at the fate of their Savior. But Simon, jostled occasionally by the hordes, cared nothing for Jesus or his suffering. He could not tear his eyes from Dismas. In front of Simon lay Dismas, crucifying. The muscles of his hard body were drawn taut. His soiled loin cloth rested loosely over his hips. His head was thrown back; the tendons of his neck bulged. Tears streamed down his dirt-stained face. Vainly, Dismas sought to lighten his own weight and stop the pain of the nails. In the throes of his pain, Dismas bowed his head and, with tears streaming down his face, starred into Simon's eyes. Those eyes, filled with unendurable suffering, burned into Simon's soul. In midst of the madness, Simon reached out his right hand and touched the feet of Dismas, who recoiled, hopelessly shifting his weight, trying to alleviate his own suffering. Simon kept his hand on Dismas' warm foot, then pulled it back to stare at the small pool of blood running into his palm. Suddenly bumped from behind, Simon stumbled forward and fell against Dismas' legs. The blood splattered down Simon's hands and onto his arms. Dismas moaned in agony. Simon again looked up at Dismas, who wept and writhed in pain. Simon too was weeping, half from desire, half from despair at Dismas' fate. He slid to his knees before Dismas, reaching up. But the guards pulled Simon away, back into the multitude.

What happened then remains a blur. Simon heard the calm, soft voice of Jesus, the screams of the women and the laughter from the multitude. He even saw Dismas say something to the other thief and then to Jesus. Blood and its smell had filled the air and maddened the already frenzied crowd.

Stopping in front of a large, mahogany door, Simon pulled a set of keys out of his pants pocket, slipped one into the lock and turned it. The door opened slowly. The smell of fresh blood crept into his nostrils. The sound of whimpering and low moans drifted out of the darkness. Simon reached to his right, found the dimmer switch and slowly slid it up. Muted light, emanating from recesses in the walls as well as the ceiling, cascaded down the long, silent corridor before him. Numerous crosses, with young men crucifying on them, leaned against both sides of the corridor.

These were the first born sons of the multitude.

The initial massacre of the first born sons of the multitudes, elders and priests began several days after the original crucifixion. It began with a few young men, mere faces in the crowd. It also included a priest. Their bodies were found, laid out in the Field of Blood. For this, a potter's field, was the land bought by the priests and elders with the money Judas had returned to them.

Over the centuries the slaughter, now quieter, continued. Tracked, found and studied for his weaknesses—money, sex, drugs or power—each had been seduced by his own desires or, as necessary, abducted. Retribution against the descendants of the multitude always occurred during Lent. Revenge against the descendants of the priests and the elders occurred on Easter.

These young men who hung before Simon were the first born sons of the multitude, the ones who, as Jesus dragged his cross to his own death, laughed, cheered and shouted, "Let him be crucified!"

Simon never made it to the end of the hallway without an erection. Tonight, as he did most nights, he paused in front of a young man, raised his eyes and gazed at the spectacle before him. The young man's head was turned slightly upward and to the side, expos-ing his long, sinewy neck. Tears, glistening under the lights, trickled down his face. The smooth, hairless chest heaved in slow, exhausted sobs. His long legs were crossed at his feet, his cock resting against his slender thighs. Simon's breathing deepened and slowed. His cock hardened. Instinctively he reached out his hand and placed it on the young man's slender waist. The youth stirred, responding to Simon's touch. Almost imperceptibly, the young man released a low moan and shifted his body, trying vainly to relieve the suffering caused by the nails in his feet and hands. Slowly Simon moved his hand over the young man's ass, then gently trailed his fingers down the young man's thigh. Half way down, Simon dug his nails deep into the boy's flesh. The youth arched his back, whimpered and tried to pull away from the pain. Simon smiled, his cock now rock hard. His fingers released the youth's flesh and trailed softly down the young man's leg. When he reached the youth's calf, Simon moved his hand around to the back of the leg and ran it down to the heel where it rested briefly. Blood dripped slowly into his palm. After a few moments, Simon pulled back his hand and gazed at the blood filling his palm and spilling over the edges of his fingers. Simon lifted his hand and watched the glistening pool of liquid run down his arm. Then he turned and continued down the corridor, his heartbeat his only companion.

By now, Dismas would already have brought his young man into the bedroom, sucked him off and fed him more drugs and booze.

Simon arrived at the end of the corridor and stood in front of a large, heavy door. He closed his eyes, took a deep breath and reached for the doorknob. Suppressing a desire to vomit, he quietly opened the door and stepped in. The room was cool, the slate floor immac-ulate as were the stone walls. Completely bare, except for a candle casting dim, flickering shadows across the walls, the space had a silence like that of a monastery, a place that knew only whispers.

"Simon, my child," hissed a voice to Simon's right. A long, fleshy arm, covered with aging, sagging skin reached out from the dark-ness. Simon flinched at the touch, recovered and stiffly leaned over and kissed the hand of Mary, who sat on a cushion on the floor, wrapped, as always, in her dark shawls and robes.

"Do I frighten you, my child?" she whispered as she tightened her grip on Simon's wrist and pulled him closer. Instinctively, Simon breathed through his mouth. It was the only way he could decrease the noxious smell that emanated from Mary's body. His face was within inches of her. She raised an icy, dry hand and cradled his cheek. She studied his face and downcast eyes.

"Simon, do you love me?" she asked as she stroked his cheek and searched his face. She always asked this question of him. Simon pulled back slightly, pried her hand off his and, after patting it, returned it to her lap.

"Of course," he said curtly, lying as he always did. As he talked, he smoothed her robes. Women, in all their femaleness, disgusted Simon. They always had. Filled with dark, moist places and bodily mysteries that horrified him, women completely repulsed Simon. His involvement with Mary continued simply because she was, and always had been, his only access to Dismas. It was she who summoned Dismas back from the dead; it was she who begged Simon to stay with her; it was she who promised Simon anything—access to young men, power—anything he desired if he would only stay at her side and help her revenge the death of Jesus, her only son. That night Simon agreed to be Mary's companion. He would, and did, agree to everything she asked of him just to be with Dismas one more time. To touch his body, to bind his wounds, to witness his suffering and then lie beside him and alleviate his own suffering, Simon would—and did—agree to anything Mary asked.

"How are you my son?" Mary asked, settling back on her cushion. She slipped her hand onto Simon's thigh. Mary's physical intimacy, something she took even further with Dismas, who did not seem to care and in fact sought it out, revolted Simon. Equally repulsive was Mary's relationship with Jesus, which Simon had witnessed before Jesus' death. The sensuality she had oozed when with Jesus, and his inability to separate from her, filled Simon with revulsion. The way she touched Jesus, stroking his hair, whispering in his ear, was loathsome to witness. She was more like his lover than his mother.

Simon knelt beside Mary and moved a candle closer to her cushion. The light illuminated her sunken eyes and withered face.

Simon paused in his ministrations and turned just in time to see the door behind him slowly open. Before them stood Dismas, with the body of the young man draped across his arms. The youth was shirtless, his body lying limply in Dismas' arms. The youth's khaki pants were partially unbuttoned, exposing his flesh down to the start of his pubic line. Briefly, Simon's gaze met Dismas' from the doorway. Behind Simon, Mary whimpered with desire. He stepped aside. Mary's arms were outstretched; a look of child-like idiocy consumed her face. As Dismas walked towards her, she whimpered again, now wriggling her hands and fingers, motioning him to approach. Doing as directed, Dismas took several steps forward, knelt and laid the unconscious young man in Mary's arms. Then he stepped back and took his place next to Simon, their hips touching slightly.

Mary licked her lips and slowly moved her left hand over the youth's face, then down his neck and onto his chest. Briefly her hand hovered over the youth's crotch. Then she wrapped both arms around the young man and pulled his limp body to her chest. Slowly, she rocked the still-warm body, moaning softly. Tears trickled down her cheeks. She slowly and gently ran her fingers through the youth's hair and trailed her fingertips over his soft, full lips. When her hand reached the boy's throat, she slid it beneath his neck and pulled the boy's face directly up to hers, studying the visage of this descendant of a Golgothan priest. Rage mixed with a smile slithered over her features. She slid her right hand over the top of the youth's skull and positioned her fingers directly over his eyelids. "This is my body," she hissed and sunk her fingers directly into the youth's eye sockets. Blood oozed out of them. She clamped her powerful arm around his head. "THIS IS MY BLOOD," she spat out and sank her teeth into the boy's neck—and fed.

Wet

M. CHRISTIAN

The brush was dry so he wet it.

The strokes at first were always, for some reason, slow and precise. He knows that nothing will remain of them after it's done, but for some reason it always starts that way: bands, shades of the same color, going vertical, diagonal, horizontal. He guesses, when he does think about the act, that it is a getting acquainted with the brushes, the canvas—his medium.

Why that should be when he has painted for so very long is a mystery Doud never examined.

Dry again—silent, precise strokes now skittering and scratching across the smooth face of the canvas. *Dries so quickly.* He wet the brush again.

Those first strokes were a climb into the work, he supposes when he does. Painting those stripes, bands of one color—always that one color—are like the rungs of a ladder. Going up, into the act, the glow, of creativity…of making a work.

The next movements of the brush were wild, feverish: all precise control lost in the rising swell of what was fleeting around his mind, just beyond Doud's normal vision. He knew, certainly, absolutely, that he was trying to pin it down now with the brush, the color—to make it stick and stay so he can see it clearly: see if it is pretty or ugly.

Dry again. He dipped it into his seemingly inexhaustible well and continued.

Maybe a man. Yes, perhaps that: like a stroller walking out of a fog, a shape becoming shoulders, a broad chest, legs, and what could be a waist. Then, with more movements of the brush, it grew details like leaves from a tree: The curves of a chest, the tendons in the arms, the contours of muscles and bone, the texture of smooth skin…a face.

Dry again. Doud dipped the brush into his red-filled mouth and tried to capture the man more fully.

The street was brilliant with a heaven of shines and reflections from a light rain. The primary neon colors burst from places like Jackson's Hole, the Ten Pin, the 87 Club, Aunt Mary's Diner, hit the street, the sidewalk, the faces of the tall buildings like…like *watercolors,* Doud thought, though his own medium was a lot less flowing and fluid.

The Space didn't have neon, and despite the beauty of the rainshellacked street outside, the owner would never ever ponder lighting his very nondescript doorway with its gaudy attraction. Wellington took extremely cool pride in the austerity of his gallery—going over its rubber-tiled steps, eggshell walls, industrial lighting, stainless steel display stands and single office countertop with an eye as precise and chilly as a level. Doud easily imagined him thinking the photographs, paintings and sculptures that paid his rent a distraction from the purity of an absolutely empty room.

He hoped for a frozen second that the flash had been lighting beyond the window, out among the glimmering night street and its hunched and brisk people.

Doud loved the rain and especially lightning. Like the bands of slow, precise color that started his works, he never really examined why the world being lit for a second, frozen and trapped in a blink of pure silver, fascinated him. Maybe it was the raw power of natural electricity—or maybe it was just the close comfort of being snug and warm for the evening that he associated with rain outside: Lightning was the tiger prowling outside while he warmed his feet, safe and warm, inside.

But lightning doesn't come from within (unless you count inspiration): Trapped with the flash, for a second, was his own face in the window glass: wide, large brown eyes, aquiline nose, brushy brows; curled black hair; deeply tanned and lined skin; large, strong mouth with hidden teeth. Some thought him Italian, others American or East Indian. A few guessed at maybe Eskimo or even Polynesian. Never guessed the truth of New York (son of New Yorkers). Never, ever, guessed his age.

The disappointment over a lightning-free night came quick, a gentle slap (because it was a simple pleasure) and he turned back to the semi-crowded gallery. There he was, a too-clean-looking photographer he instantly knew was either the friend of an artist or one of them himself (newspaper shooters were usually a lot more scruffy and exotic). Doud hated to be photographed, hated being frozen in time and having his image in the hands of, and at the mercy of, someone else.

"Yours?" the photographer asked, his face opaqued by the complex of a flash unit, massive lens and a matte-black camera body. Dirty blond, almost brown, tall, broad—was all Doud could see.

"Those are," Doud said, nodding to the right-hand wall and the five paintings that were edge-on and so just the colors of their frames. Doud didn't need to see them, an artist's privilege of many hours of work.

The camera came down and he treated Doud with his profile as he scanned the paintings: pale, hollow cheeks; bones seemingly as thin as a bird's; wet blue eyes that, even across the mostly empty gallery, seemed to see far too much, far too quickly; a mouth that bloomed with lips that Doud found himself instantly wanting to kiss; a nose all but invisible against the beauty of his face (which was fine, having such a profound nose, Doud disliked the same in others); and a fine and elegant body that seemed to be all chest and shoulders, a rack on which thin, pale arms and legs dangled with a refined and dignified posture. He was dressed simply in black pants, a very tight turtleneck and an elegant, and probably antique, morning coat—a direct polar extreme from Doud's old sweatshirt, boots and jeans.

It was a kind of shock to see someone who sported himself so...*dapper* was a word that came out of Doud's memory along with the smell of horses and raw electricity, the rumble of the El trains, and scratchy Al Jolson from a gramophone. Dapper? Yes, refined and polished. Quite out of character for The Space and being an admirer of Doud's work.

"You probably get asked this a lot—" the man started to say, fixing those darting, grinning eyes on Doud and smiling pure warmth.

"An awful lot," Doud said with a practiced sigh that spoke of a joke rather than true exasperation. "Animals," he finished, answering the question.

"I saw the jar," the photographer said, indicating with a jerk of his camera the large bell jar stuffed with a cow's severed head on the floor in front of Doud's wall, "and thought as much."

"*The medium is the message,*" Doud said with a smile. "People either look at me real funny and think about DNA testing or they think it's a trick of paint and technique."

"It is rather…your studio must really stink."

Doud laughed, the sound coming from down deep, "Lots of windows, and I keep my stuff well-covered. Then of course I fix it real good after. Lots of shellac."

The man smiled, shifted his camera and stuck out a pale, long-boned hand, "Jona. Jona Periliak."

"Charmed," Doud said. Jona's hand was dry and very warm, almost hot. "Are you here as well, or just taking shots for a friend?"

"I'm in the backroom."

Doud remembered the photographs on his way in that evening, but since he never supervised his installations he hadn't looked beyond that initial glance. "Would you mind," Doud said, smiling his best smile and hoping he'd remembered to gargle and brush his teeth, "showing me?"

The Space had started to fill up since they'd been talking. The usual wine and cheese crowd of artists and their usual mixture of friends. They carefully passed by suits and jeans and piercings and Doc Martens and even a latex bodysuit and a full tux.

The backroom was sky blue, lit with Wellington's usual baby spots. Maybe a dozen, maybe fourteen, black and white portraits. Jona looking thoughtful with glasses and a book. Jona looking sad with gravestones in the background. Jona looking pained as blood, black as ink (and it could have been) ran down from a sliced palm. Jona excited, his bare chest slick with sweat and probably oil. Doud scanned them all, lingering long over excited and pained, giving them his examining look—then glanced over at the title of the series: *Portrait of the Artists.*

Doud hated photographs: He saw them as a kind of cheat, a kind of shortcut.

"They're fine—" Doud said, using a word that also came from penny candy and hoop skirts. He didn't like photographs for lots of reasons, but Jona was very pretty, very striking in his pallor and funereal garb. Being self-portraits made it easy to lie—Jona was very fine, indeed.

"You don't like them." He didn't seem hurt at all, more like he was calling Doud on his politeness.

"I didn't say that. It's not my medium is all. Besides, I meant what I said. I like the way these are all parts of you."

"I appreciate that," Jona said, moving the camera behind him so Doud could have a nice view of his flat stomach and hard chest—

at least what he could see outlined in the black turtleneck.

It had been a long time for Doud. He could barely remember the face, and couldn't, for the life of him, think of the last name of the last person he was attracted to as much as he was attracted to Jona. *You'd think,* he found himself thinking with surprising clarity, *after all this time I'd get better at this.* At least he wasn't hungry—but he did feel that other kind of desperation, the one that wanted to make his gently shaking hands reach up and stroke Jona's soft, pale cheeks and tell him how beautiful he looked. *Go on,* he thought next, *say that you appreciate him....*

"Are you—" Doud did say, waving at the row of photographs, "—going to be here long?"

"Tonight or the show?" and before Doud could respond either way, Jona quickly added, "Just a few minutes and the end of the month."

The Space had started to fill up and Doud felt himself being pulled by their body heat, their eyes. Going to an opening was rare, staying as late as he had was ever rarer...but Jona, and Jona's beautiful attention, was priceless.

But the people—

"It's kind of getting crowded," the pale beauty said, with a smile that made a warm spot on Doud's stomach and made his eyes lose focus for a second.

Doud heard himself say, "Let's go outside."

Doud liked the ships and the trains. And the rent was cheap. He could understand why others didn't like living next to the yards, in front of the bay, especially when one of the big diesel engines revved at one a.m. or a tramp steamer blasted its departure at two.

Despite being jerked awake too damned early in the morning, Doud liked living in the shadow of the simple, huge machines. People made him feel alone and way too unique, outside always looking in and...hungry. The boats and the trains made him feel practically human by comparison.

"You never said why you didn't like my shots," Jona said, sitting on Doud's comfortable burgundy sofa, twirling a glass quarter-full of white wine.

"I guess I think it's a cheat—"

"That it takes a lot less to handle a camera than a brush? Not necessarily—" Jona started to say, leaning forward to look into Doud's eyes.

Doud looked away so quickly it made his head hurt for a moment. "You never asked why I paint the way I do," he said to his spiraling red and blue rug.

"I thought it had something to do with the cycle of death—you know, something growing from something dying. Your pictures from dead cows."

Doud found himself frowning: another person who didn't pick up on it. He wondered why he had any kind of following at all, or was it just that people liked seeing paintings done in blood just on principle? "No," he said, refilling his glass even though he knew he'd had way too much already (he got drunk so damned quickly), "that's not really it. I do it to give them something close to immortality."

Jona was rapt. In many ways more rapt than he should be. "But you don't like photographs."

Doud sighed, hated saying these kinds of things but also tired of lying. Yeah, at the time it usually got him company for the night, or even a weekend, but he didn't like how he felt in the morning, on Monday. At least when he told the truth—well, mostly the truth— he liked the company he always ended up keeping: Doud. "Nothing lasts forever," he finally said after a long damned silence (god, Jona was pretty), "except for a photograph. Throw the negative away, then maybe a print will age and fade away naturally. Won't last absolutely forever. I paint because the...animals will last so much longer. Not forever, just a lot, lot longer."

Jona smiled and sipped his own wine. "You don't like forever?"

Doud shook his head, slow and tired: the sound of iron wheels on cobblestones, opium, a harbor full of sails, coal.... "Nothing ever is. A long, long time...yes. But not forever. Nothing is ever forever."

Jona thought for a long time, twirling his wine in his glass in what Doud knew instantly could be a very annoying habit. Then he put the glass down carefully on Doud's spiraling rug and started to dig in a cotton shoulder bag he had brought from The Space. He came up with a stiff manila envelope and, never once meeting Doud's eyes, undid the clasp and removed a sandwich of gray cardboard. Between them:

A City street in a copy of plate sepia; carriage bus filigreed with advertisements for patent medicines and Clothiers for Fine, Respected Gentlemen; women in hoop skirts, men with top hats and swallow-tail coats; children in sailor suits, pinafores and button-up shoes; to one side,

in a wool coat and a simple bowler, a man with a casual, caught-unawares face: handsome eagle nose, dark features that could be Italian, Mediterranean, East Indian....
I hate photographs, Doud thought hollowly, coldly.

Jona sat in a little coffee house, the Kona Coast, and kept Doud's words circulating in his mind, trying to keep them fresh, trying not to loose a scrap.

His lips and throat hurt. Getting up that morning, he'd coughed up a fat, dark slug of phlegm and blood into Doud's bathroom sink. By noon his lips were a faded purple and it hurt to smile.

Kona Coast wasn't his first choice, something less loaded would have been much better, but he didn't seem to have any room in his mind to think of someplace new, original: Jeffrey's favorite place would have to do.

It's painful till you get used to it. Let your body acclimate to its new design.

He felt good. Damned good. The world was sharp and clean and crisp. Looking across the tiny coffee house he felt his attention glide like a scalpel across the wooden tables, the stacks of free newspapers, the walls decorated years thick with roommate-wanted, jobs-offered, bands-playing, films-showing flyers and handbills. Someone walked in and for a second, not even a heartbeat, he thought it was Jeffrey, but with his new focus, his new clean eyes, he saw that the face across the room was not even close. This man had gray at his temples. Jeffrey had been too vain to allow even a single aging hair in his own.

That *almost seeing* irritated Jona. It pissed him off to have Jeffrey come into his thoughts now, when he was trying to hold everything in, to keep it bottled up, commit it to hard memory.

Am I the only one? I guess I might be. I've made...friends like you a few times. You get lonely, and it's hard to get close to your food—at least emotionally. I don't know if they've managed to make...friends like I can. I don't think they can.

I don't know if I'm a myth or a fluke. I was born this way.

Looking into his coffee, Jona caught and captured the wisps of steam, freezing them with his mind as Doud's words echoed around the chit-chat of the coffee house. At first he had been too excited, and in too much pain, to hear clearly what Doud was saying. But there, in the Kona Coast, the scene had come back to Jona, the words, moving in front of him like the steam from his white and sweet coffee.

Two things. Remember the two things of what you are now. I give you one but not the other: Murder. Immortality.

Again, Jeffrey intruded on Jona's recollection of Doud: Jeffrey standing in front of him again. Another fight. Another argument. Jeffrey's shock and outrage over something Jona had said or done. That outrage—it made Jona furious. Jeffrey's blank, shocked look, his wet eyes, as he tried to understand why Jona had done what he'd done. Didn't matter what he'd done—said something catty, made some remark, flirted with someone's partner, fucked someone's partner, stolen some useless knick-knack—there was Jeffrey's smug, shining face whipping Jona with just a disappointed look. He hated Jeffrey when he looked at him like that. Hated his boring superiority.

Like I said, I don't know what I am. Many things, labels, work but mostly they don't. Sunlight doesn't hurt, crosses don't do anything, stakes will—but then they'll probably kill anything. I have to eat twice, sometimes only once, if I take it easy, every six months. I can do more, but don't.

The photograph. Jona remembered the context with an electric flash. Some friend of Jeffrey's, a smug little queen with an arrogant love and dedication to antiques. The little shit was too in love with his partner, an ebony beauty named Tan, to respond to Jona's come-on so he'd compensated by lifting an album of turn-of-the-century photographs.

Jeffrey had found out, of course, and had shown up at Jona's little Park Circle studio to demand the book back.

Seeing his ex-lover standing in his front room and looking down at him like dirt that had somehow managed to stick to Jeffrey's pristine shoes, Jona had been softly quaking with anger. "Do you see it here?" he'd said, trying not to betray his fury.

"I know you took it, Jo," Jeffrey had said.

"If you can find it, then call me a fucking thief. If you don't see it, then get the fuck out."

He'd never looked, just left saying that he didn't want to know Jona anymore.

After he'd done…whatever it was that Doud had done, he had put Jona, heaving, panting, and vibrating like a junkie, on his couch, dried and not dried blood like paste all over his face and chest and mouth.

Doud had been crying, almost puking with the tears dribbling from his large eyes: "I'm so sorry. So sorry. I just want some company. It's stupid. I'm so stupid. I don't know you. Don't know you at all—"

In the book, photographs. In one of the photographs, a man he recognized from an upcoming installation at The Space. The medium and the perfect likeness: He didn't really think anything about it, didn't really put anything together about it, aside from another game, another trick. Show Doud the shot, freak the fuck out of him and pick up the pieces as he'd done so many times before.

With Jeffrey, it had been games of fucking anything that moved—especially when Jeffrey liked to "bond" with his lovers. Easy to dick with someone who just wants you—you fuck someone else.

"You have to, but you don't have to enjoy it. I do it. I do it but I try to atone as best I can. I make it quick, I don't enjoy it. I don't do it for any reason than to survive. And…yes, I try to make it up to them somehow: make them special for their donation of time to me."

Doud had been standing in front of one of his paintings, running his elegant fingers over the five sharp, clear lines that cut vertically through the otherwise unmarked canvas.

I promise you a long, long life. I promise you almost immortality. I promise you my company. That's all.

The doors to the little coffee house opened again, and Jona's steam, and the scene in his mind, vanished in the cool breeze. Glancing up, he saw with his new, crystal vision a tall, slender man with shoulder-length brown curls without a trace of gray.

"Jeffrey," Jona said, motioning him over to his table.

"What do you want, Jona?" Jeffrey asked, walking over but standing stiff and straight.

"Have something to tell you—" Jona said.

"Is it about Abbott's book? If you have it, you should get it back to him. I don't want to see it, know about it, or have anything to do with you."

"Jeffrey," Jona said, with a spark of playful warmth in his voice, "don't you think you owe me at least a little chance, a tiny one, to end this well? I don't want you to hate me, Jeffrey."

"Is it the book, Jona?" It was rare to see Jeffrey almost angry. Fury crashed through Jona like a metal wave, and he tasted copper in his mouth and on his bruised and swollen lips.

But then Jona firmly recalled Doud, the kiss, the new self in him, the new world he was about to walk into, and so he said, smiling despite his very painful lips: "Yes, Jeffrey, it's the book. But much more. Come back to my place and I'll tell you all about it."

Jona had slept the night before, his face and mouth wet with blood, in Doud's bed. As the sun started to burn up the city, he had gotten cleaned up and gone straight to the Kona Coast for thought and coffee. Then Jeffrey.

Though Jeffrey was a few inches taller than gaunt and hallow-cheeked Jona, he seemed smaller, somehow, as if the night, Doud and the blood had added to him. A lot.

Jeffrey tagged along as Jeffrey always did, a few steps behind, scanning the dim and damp streets from the coffee house to Jona's place. They didn't talk much: the silence between them was a hard wall of skewed viewpoints. Jeffrey felt betrayed by Jona, deceived and manipulated too many times.

Jona looked back over his shoulder at him. His viewpoint was…simpler: *I like looking down on you, Jeffrey. There is so little to you, really. So very little. Just like everyone else. So very little.*

"I don't really want to come up," Jeffrey said, standing on the slick marble of the foyer as Jona clinked and rattled his keys.

"But you want it, don't you?" Jona said, opening the door and stepping aside.

"I want closure to this, Jo," Jeffrey said, shouldering past and starting up the two flights to Jona's apartment.

"Well, so do I," Jona said, from behind him, as he closed the door.

Another rattle of keys, another door, again Jeffrey stepped in first, scanning the apartment slowly, even though nothing had changed since he'd last been there. Closing the door behind him, Jona smiled wide and broad against the thud of pain from his lips—caught up in a kind of laugh that was coming from deep inside. It had sprung from a kind of giddy relief that he could see Jeffrey clearly, very clearly, for the first time.

So little to you, Jeffrey. So damned little. And to think I envied you, your grace and meticulous gestures. Your subtle humor. Your gliding hands. I loved to make you…all of you, do what I wanted. Cry. Laugh. Get so frustrated. Now I don't need to.

Now I'm much more.

"Can I have a kiss, Jeffrey?" Jona said softly, trying to hide the laughter that wanted to explode out of him as he put a careful, gentle hand on Jeffrey's high shoulder.

"Jona," Jeffrey started to say, shaking his head against being struck suddenly sad by the tone in Jona's voice.

"I just want something to close all this. A kiss would be perfect. Perfect. Then the photograph. I promise."

"Always playing fucking games," Jeffrey's voice was level and smooth, crisp and elegant, as always, but Jona knew that he was furious, that he was shaking with anger beneath his cultivated image. "No more hoops, Jona. You're not in love with me. You never were. You're not anything you pretended to be. I saw you, Jona. I saw you when you dicked us all around and played with my head. When you fucked around. Smiling. Always fucking smiling."

"So I don't even deserve a good-bye kiss?" Jona asked, trying desperately not to smile.

The rain was cold, and, of course, wet, but his concentration on the one window dimmed it down to the gentle stings of the drops in his eyes. He didn't blink. Didn't need to. Doud stood in a short alley reeking of vomit and urine and watched the shadows moving against a hard light. Didn't need to blink, could now find Jona anywhere in the city: There were other things he could do, but, frankly, he rarely had a need for them.

How many times? Doud thought, looking down at the sparkling streets for a second, listening to the hush of the passing cars, moving through a night frozen at moments with lightning flashes. He was out and about, walking with the tiger of a storm when he should have been home and warm. It was something he'd done before: *How many times have I stood like this and waited? How many times have I stood here, knowing I'd be alone again in a few hours?*

But there was a little hope in the back of his mind, a little glow, the same little glow that had always accompanied those other thoughts: *maybe just this once.*

The heat from Jeffrey was like a open flame in Jona's face. It rolled off him in waves of luxurious warmth. Jona was normally a blackout kisser, letting his eyes squeeze shut with the concentration of a good kiss, rolling in the play of tongue and lips and teeth. But his eyes were wide open now—wide and capturing Jeffrey as he bent down the few inches to kiss him, catching the tiny pores on the end of what he'd always thought of as a perfect nose. He saw the tiny broken blood vessels in his eyes; the silken bags under his eyes that would get worse with age; a hint of wine and garlic on his breath that meant that tall, elegant Jeffrey had been haunting one of his goth friends for company. Jona took him in with a glance and a breath in the moment Jeffrey relaxed to kiss. Jona didn't see, for once, the statue who had deemed Jona good in bed and worthy of his debonair company.

Jona saw bone and sweat and piss and shit and muscle and guts and the raging, boiling inferno of quarts and quarts of blood.

Jona's cock was iron, steel in his pants. He wanted to reach down and stroke it, rub himself to a nice orgasm as he held himself there, high above the simple meat of the man he'd thought of as perfect, idolized. He wanted to orgasm from just standing there—the ego rush of realizing what Jeffrey really was and what Jona was now. His cock raged full and hard and straining with the pure power of being someone else at last, at being powerful at last.

Kiss me.

The touch was a shock. Jona was so focused, so drawn into his perception of the puppet, the hunk of gristle that was Jeffrey, that he didn't expect the touch to be silken and sparked with tension. He jerked back a tiny amount, breaking the contact as quickly as it had been made. He expected something rough and coarse to match his meaty revelation about his old flame.

Well, he thought, smiling against his painful lips and moving even closer, *rabbits feel nice, too.*

The touch was softer this time and the two old lovers fell into the comfort of each other's bodies. Jeffrey might have wanted something chaste and simple, a gothic rite of departure like a Victorian greeting card ("Nice to have known your acquaintance") but the jungle fury that was suddenly flickering in and out of Jona washed the practiced distance right out of him. It was like Jeffrey'd been submerged in a powerful electric current and his body was jerking along to it—despite his poised mentality.

It was a good kiss. A fine kiss. It was a lover's kiss at the height of their attraction.

It didn't seem like a kiss good-bye.

As Jona started, Jeffrey's cock went from a strong erection to a painful hardness in his precise pants. It was the first indication that Jona had started it right. He was surprised by how natural, how easy it felt. He'd thought, as he'd asked for the kiss, that it might be hard, that he might even have to resort to another way. But it was like the comfort of…a lover's kiss. Jona just followed the way that seemed right and it all just flowed along with the simple determination of any biological function. Like kissing, like drinking, like swallowing, like eating.

Like breathing. Jona kissed Jeffrey and started to breathe him in. Gently at first, but then stronger and stronger. Jeffrey liked it, liked the strong suction of Jona's mouth on his, liked the earthy pull of his lungs on his own.

Then he tasted blood and his chest started to hurt.

The kiss climbed up from the edge hard passion of rough sex, of their cocks pressing—dueling clubs between their frenzied bodies. It went from that flash of painful sex to pure pain to screaming.

But Jeffrey couldn't scream, Jona's mouth was over his and he was pulling Jeffrey inside-out through his own throat.

Jona felt Jeffrey's pure, hot blood boil up and out of him and down his throat. He pulled and tugged with his breath and the other of his new self. Jona reached down with his hunger and pulled Jeffrey out of himself. The blood and essence was a scalding wine of life splashing against his lips, teeth, gums and tongue. He wanted to laugh, to scream, his joy and power to the moon, to the sun, but more than that, more than anything he wanted *more*. He wanted the totality of the meat and blood (oh, yes, the *blood*) of Jeffrey. He wanted to drink him to the last drop, to pull him all the way in, to drink him through their kiss till there was nothing more to hold, to stroke—till Jeffrey's threatening perfection was nothing but a slaughterhouse residue.

Jona's cock was iron, something fundamental and material in the torrent of life that he was pulling out of Jeffrey. He wanted to fuck something, anything. He wanted to drive his spur of metal into a worthy, powerful lover.

He thought of Doud. He thought of the little man in the jeans and the sweater. Doud had stopped, had held back just enough of Jona— then had forced the blood, water, tears, cum, meat back into him. He'd tasted Jona, and put him back into his, now changed, body.

He could do the same, he guessed, with Jeffrey—but he didn't want to. Didn't want to at all. He was hungry and thirsty and Jeffrey just...tasted too damned good.

In his arms, Jeffrey screamed into his mouth and diminished in stature. Jona pulled the fluids out of him, drew the essence and blood out of him and down Jona's throat. Hypnotized, Jona watched Jeffrey's skin darken and lose its shine—replaced by a matte powder; Jona saw blindness glaze over Jeffrey's eyes as the fluid was drawn back into his skull, into his throat and into Jona. He saw Jeffrey's cheeks concave and his bones start to snap from the pressure, the spreading dryness.

Soon (too soon!) Jona was holding him, the child-sized husk of Jeffrey, the dusty bag of whining, chalk-soft bones and papery skin.

Still he pulled and pulled. Jeffrey snapped and tore and crackled like a low fire, or paper being crumpled. The last drop tasted of music: a single high note that passed his teeth and dropped like a bell into Jona's stomach, body.

There was little left of elegant Jeffrey: an ancient doll of hair, scraps of skin, fingernails, and shattered bones like dice in a bag. Not enough to identify—easily buried or flushed down the toilet.

Jona put the dry fragments of Jeffrey down on the floor and stretched, feeling the blood surge and roll in his strong body, feeling it start to mix and burn with his own. He felt exalted, added to, charged—

Full.

Jeffrey rolled in the back of his throat, a warm wine filling him, draining into him. He caught a steaming reflection in one of the windows and laughed at himself. *Friends sometimes leave an impression on you,* he thought to his normal, slender reflection. *Jeffrey, I guess, didn't on me.*

Doud was watching an engine back into the yards when his doorbell rang. He'd known it would—soon enough—but it seemed to have happened faster than he had expected.

Going to the door, he absently checked to make sure his hat, coat and shoes weren't anywhere in sight. His wet hat, coat and shoes.

"Come in," he said to a dripping Jona. Behind him, cars kicked up ripples of inch-deep rainwater as they furrowed through reflections of industrial lighting, "I've missed you."

"I like that," Jona said, entering and shaking his coat off before handing it to Doud, "People don't usually miss me."

"I did. I've missed you for a long time. Longer than today, even."

"Been a long time?" Jona said from the front room, looking back at Doud hanging up his coat, the words sinking into him. "I guess it has."

"Very long. It's hard to relate to others. You should find that out quickly. It's just the two of us."

"Intimate," Jona said, sitting down on the couch. "I like intimate. Just the two of us against the world."

"The world would win, don't forget. Drink?"

"Sure."

As Doud rattled and banged in the kitchen, Jona called: "How long, Doud?"

"What do you mean?"

"I mean, how long."

"No, I mean how long for what? How long have I been this way? Forever. I told you: born this way. Since I got laid? A month ago this Thursday, in the afternoon. Since I've had real…companionship? Twenty years, give or take two or three years. Since I killed someone for food? Seven months ago."

"Do you like this, Doud?" Jona said from the door to the kitchen. There was something in his voice, in the tone if not the words. It wasn't a deep ponder or a frightened seek for answers. Not laughter, not excitement—nothing so obvious. Not even a smile.

Close, though. Close to a smile.

"I don't have a choice. You have a cut cock, Jona—do you miss that inch or two of skin? You miss that much more than I miss the rest of them outside. I have always been this way. Always. I don't know what they are really like, all those people out there. I just know what I am, and what I have to do to live…for as long as I have."

"But you're not one of them."

"I'm something. Something that needs to suck 'em bone dry to survive. So I have to keep myself distant from them—" Doud said, handing Jona a simple white wine in a cheap glass. "Can't have cows as friends, you know."

"Is that how you really see them?"

"No. I don't. But they're not what I am. I miss someone I can talk to, share my life with. Be with when the 'otherness' is everywhere. I do what I have to do to keep living, but that's all. It's enough, though, to keep them out there and me in here."

"Well," Jona said, knocking back half of his glass with one swallow, "it's not you anymore. It's us."

Gesturing him back to the front room, Doud smiled softly, small and quick, saying, "I appreciate that. I do."

"I appreciate you, Doud: what you've given me."

"It...almost makes it worthwhile, to be able to see people grow up. Buggies to Neil Armstrong. Typhus and children's bars to Apple and the Web."

Smiling, Jona sat down next to Doud on the couch. "I'm looking forward to it. I'm really—" *smiling* "—looking forward to it."

"I'm glad you are," Doud said. "I'm glad."

Time dragged for a few minutes as they sipped their wine. As it often happens, their heat was a magnet. First, they sat in uncomfortable, hard silence. Then they were closer, touching cotton pants to jeans. The temperature for both was clearly higher. Doud's hand ended up on Jona's knee. Thinking about it later, Doud thought that he probably (since he usually did) was talking, maintaining an empty patter of god-knew what: stories of elevated trains, "shooting the moon," coonskin coats, outdoor plumbing, The Yellow Kid, short pants, a woman's "well-turned ankle"—a smoke screen of articulated memories hiding his fear of the temperature between them.

Finally, Jona leaned over and kissed him.

Doud's patter vanished into a low, purring moan—one that made Jona smile a painful smile in the middle of the kiss.

When they broke, Doud was smiling, too. He reached out and put a hand on Jona's hard cock, stroking it lightly, ghostly, through Jona's jeans. "No secrets, none at all."

"Wouldn't have it any other way," Jona said, stretching, leaning back till he was a length of crackling joints.

Doud's hands were almost shaking as he undid Jona's fly, pulled his pants away from his waist, revealing softly pale skin—no underwear—and hints of distant, scratchy, hairs.

They were in the space between "we're gonna do it" and "we're doing it!" Jona lifted his ass off the couch and Doud fought and struggled with his jeans till they surrendered and were jerked down to his firm thighs.

Jona's cock wasn't huge. No exaggerations: it was simply average.

A pale column of very hard meat, head a brilliant pink. Cut. Noticeably fatter at the root than the tip, despite a wide corona. It bobbed, a gentle swaying, with a creamy drop of early excitement gleaming at the tip.

"Beautiful," Doud said, wrapping his lips around Jona's cock.

It was like a pressurized bath to Jona, a silken, damp hand strong around the nerves of his cock. A quiet man, a gothic gentleman of the nights, Jona came from a tribe that prided itself on its dour, dark orgasms—he actually made a sound. As Doud kissed the tip, then licked the shaft, then dropped his warm, wet mouth over the tip and then the entire shaft of Jona's cock, Jona made a soft, all-but-inaudible, mewing sound.

It was hard for him not to come instantly.

Practice, Jona thought, smiling against his graveyard training. Lots and lots of practice. Years of practice.

Doud's mouth was more than well-trained. It was magical. It was as if Jona could feel a tongue as nimble as fingers, as strong as an ass, as precise as an eyelash. He was lost completely to Doud's tongue, teeth, palate, lips and warm saliva. It was hard for him to focus on anything save the tiny, incredible details of Doud's lips and mouth on him.

Somewhere deep inside the raging sea of Doud's expert cocksucking, a little Jona was smiling and leaning back, sketching the territory of the future in his mind, playing the angles, and seeing where he might take it.

Simple Doud. Very simple Doud. What's yours now, will be mine later: with enough time. Now I have lots of time for lots of things…lots of fun things. In there, in his thoughts, he tripped over the corpse of Jeffrey, sticks and stones in a bag of dried, vanishing skin. It was a quiet moment, remembering Jeffrey's eyes crumbling back into their sockets, his last scream vanishing into crackling bones, tearing skin—

Then he came.

It was a screaming come, a deep brass come—all horns and woodwinds. A primal orgasm that pushed, heaved and kicked its way from the base of his balls, up through the shaft of his cock and out the top, mixing and splashing in Doud's mouth and even foaming his dark lips.

Laughing, Jona leaned forward and mussed Doud's thick, curly hair. "That was incredible…"

"Not yet," Doud said, his voice unreadable as he licked the cum from Jona's still hard cock. "Not yet..."

Doud set back to work, working his mouthy magic on Jona's again. And again Jona was on the road to a shaking, squirming come—a fast trip straight down, no bends, pedal all the way to the floor. The persistence of Doud was almost frightening, almost made Jona open his eyes wide. It was so good—too good. It was frightening. It was as if Doud had somehow plugged himself directly into Jona's cock, and had just thrown a switch to make him come and come and come.

He did and did and did.

It didn't stop. One come after another, each squirt a little less than the one before, each a little less good and a little more...forced. Each one more of a strain.

Then the pain started.

Jona tried to make Doud stop but the pain was too much. It was all he could do to hang on to the couch and let the hot iron that he felt being poured down his cock come out as a deep, echoing scream. His balls felt like they were cracking, breaking apart from the pressure of Doud's suction. His cock was tearing; it was ripping inside out from the force of Doud's lips, the strength of his body reaching into Jona and pulling him out through his cock. Again and again he tried to move, to make his spasming, cramping hands let loose of the couch and bring them down on Doud to make him stop, but the cramps were like handcuffs around his wrists, around his fingers, trapping him there.

Then Doud stopped and said, with blood and cum dripping down his chin, eyes lit with fire from inside, "I promised you near forever—not a weapon, not a toy for you to enjoy. I gave you years, not murders."

Weak, Jona pushed himself off the couch, trying to speak, trying to get up and get away, but he was old, broken and drained. The muscles in his stomach and his chest were wrung tight and locked around broken bones. His cock was stuffed with needles and pins, his balls were crushed and broken—trampled underfoot. Something dripped onto the floor and his cock was wet, very wet.

"You have blood on your lips you know—" Doud said, wiping his mouth on his sleeve. Then he bent down and kissed Jona hard. Very hard.

It started almost soft, almost like a kiss hello, a kiss good-bye, but then became the same special kiss that Doud had given Jona, had blessed him with. But it didn't stop where Doud had stopped before, it didn't change, mix and reverse. It went on and on and on...a kiss good-bye, like the kiss Jona had given Jeffrey.

Blood boiled up through the bursting, boiling arteries in Jona's throat. He could feel them burst like blisters, feel the blood squirt and run down into his stomach. He could feel his belly pull itself up under the power of Doud's kiss. He wanted to scream; he wanted to cough and puke and cry but he was just a straw, just a tube for his own blood boiling out of his rupturing body and into Doud.

He tried to fight, to flail against the horrible pull of Doud but his strength was laced with agony.

His eyesight was fogged with blood, then with the tearing agony of his eyeballs collapsing into themselves. Distantly, Jona felt his bones break, felt tearings and pullings deep within him and surges of fluids—burning, sweet, sour—come up his throat, into his mouth and into the vacuum of Doud.

Then all of him, all of him that was wet, did, completely, totally—and he was dead.

The brush was dry so he wet it—again.

Doud never really thought of changing mediums for his work. Never really thought about changing to, say, oils or watercolors. He knew them, had touched them here or there. But always he'd come back to the pure wet.

You have to pay your way. Long life for a long life, he thought as he started. Always the bold, straight streaks: vertical, horizontal, diagonal. The same start. Soon the canvas was a blur of dark and light reds, maybe a form there, maybe not. A foggy world seen by the light of a dying fire.

Scratch...the brush was dry. Calmly, he dipped it and fell back into the painting.

Maybe a man. Doud's strokes became bolder, firmer, as he tried to reach into that *maybe,* the potential of the work, and pull it into firmer details. A fuzzy blotch slowly started to become a head. A soft smudge started to become shoulders. Chest. Waist. Legs.

Dry again. Again, he dipped the brush into the red well of his mouth and got back to painting.

A face. Maybe someone he remembered. I promised you a long life, Jona. *I promised that you'd be around a long time.*

The brush was dry....

The Game

NANCY KILPATRICK

"Plebian idiots!" Lawrence muttered. The waiter glanced at him, plunked down the two main courses and hurried away.

"Who?" Fab asked, diving into the rigatoni in tomato sauce.

"The great, barely washed, vulgar masses, who else?"

"Well, I don't see the problem. It's just a replica."

Fab nodded at the gargoyle above the bar at *Piccolo el Diavolo* that they had been discussing. The image was not a classical one, but a modern interpretation that annoyed Lawrence. It entirely missed the point and instead of capturing evil, it became a nauseating blend of evil and good. A politically correct gargoyle!

Lawrence held up his wine glass. "No one understands the past. They think all of it led to them being born."

Fab, speaking around a mouthful of pasta, said, "Hey, it's just nostalgia. So they got it a little wrong. This is great food!"

"Nostalgia! Don't talk to me about bloody nostalgia."

While Fab ate, Lawrence lifted his goblet and stared through the glass-imitating-crystal. Always, that everyman grin slashed across Fab's generous lips, so different from Lawrence's thin, down-turned mouth. Those darker-than-dark eyes, eyes that struggled and failed to reveal only what Fab wanted them to reveal. Lawrence had trained his own pale orbs until they were masters at exposing nothing. Fab was a natural Game player, both more open and less open than almost any other "mortal" Lawrence had encountered. He liked to think of his prey as mortals because they tried his patience. And the word *human* seemed far too sentimental. In truth, though, they were all the same to him, and any man could have been sitting in Fab's chair, playing The Game.

Lawrence ignored his food and instead, while he sipped the inferior wine, stared out the window at this fragment of *rue Ste.*

Catherine. The chic restaurant was situated in the heart of the gay ghetto. Many miles of this east-west street formed a potpourri of districts, from poverty, to high commerce, to hooker, to gay, to biker and then to deeper poverty.

"How I adore *Ste. Catherine's*," he said into the glass, thinking how the street reflected his checkered past.

"Why?"

He gave Fab a meaningful look. "So many roles, *mon petit bonhomme,* so little time. At least it breaks up the ennui."

Fab laughed that silly laugh of his, the one that had obviously never touched true despair.

Lawrence, as always, picked at his linguini, too indifferent to eat, and the waiter cleared away the remnants with the usual frown and vague open-ended question not really designed to receive a negative response.

"Well, if they hadn't outlawed absinthe..." Fab said, trying, no doubt, to relate.

We'd all be dead, Lawrence thought, and drank the dregs of the sour wine.

"How much worse can it be than chartreuse?" Fab wondered absently. "Speaking of chartreuse..."

He nodded and Lawrence turned toward the door; a tall, blond drag queen named Luzanne was making An Entrance. "Don't you love it!" Fab laughed like a gleeful child.

"Where did she steal that dress?" Lawrence asked, deadpan, but he felt on automatic pilot. He'd said this line, or one just like it, and had heard it so many times....

"Isn't that the chiffon they taped around one of the floats at Gay Pride Day?"

The six-foot burly man wore a classic Dolly Parton: sequins, rhinestones, a bosomy second skin in a sickly yellow. His gestures weren't Dolly's, but then he wasn't exactly on stage at the moment. Lawrence, unlike Fab, was bored with DQs. He'd seen too many over what felt more and more like an unnaturally long span on this earth, and they were all alike. He'd even tried drag himself for a while—it lost its glamour quickly, and fucking men in skirts grew tedious. Everything had grown tedious.

They watched Luzanne prance for a while, Fab lacing the air with pithy comments, Lawrence letting his attention wander around the restaurant. Faces, familiar, even the ones he knew he hadn't seen before. Did everyone fit into a "type"? Hardcore. Precious. Window dressing. Bike Boys. Serious Leather. Transies. The odd lesbian. A leftover Fag Hag from the seventies. This was worse than a straight restaurant!

"Well, at least she left the Queen's purse at home this time!" Fab exclaimed, and tilted his head in a clownish way.

"Let's get out of here," Lawrence said.

Fab paused, batted his eyes and lifted an eyebrow. "Your wish is my command. What did you have in mind?"

"Your place."

Fab's other eyebrow lifted too. He looked startled. That was good. Catching them off guard was the best.

A dark look passed over Fab's moon face, or it could have been the shadow of the waiter bringing the bill. Lawrence had never been to Fab's apartment. He'd always avoided it, much to Fab's distress, and then when The Game turned slightly, and Fab had stopped inviting him, Lawrence began saying he wanted to visit. Fab resisted, but his heart wasn't in it, that was clear. It was pushy of Lawrence to bring it up again, since they'd just gone over this ground on the way to the restaurant. But in an instant, he realized he was crushingly bored; it was time to play this out.

Suddenly Fab threw back his head and thrust one muscular shoulder forward, Garboesque. He batted those seductive dark lashes and murmured in a throaty voice, "I vouldn't vant you to be alone!"

Lawrence said nothing, but he felt a vague regret pass through him, which quickly solidified to stone. Yes, it was definitely time to move on.

They walked along the snowy pavement of *rue la Gauchetierre,* past the tall, winding, metal staircases and wrought-iron balconies of this solidly French district where Fab lived. He was French, not Québecois, but that was about all he had ever said concerning his background. He didn't like to talk about himself and Lawrence didn't probe; he just wasn't that interested. Lawrence, of course, always lied about his past. They never knew the difference, and by the time they realized the falsehoods, it was too late.

"Remember *le Bastille?*" Fab said. More sentimental crap. This was getting better and better. He was alluding to when they met, at the baths six months ago. The attraction was non-physical from Lawrence's end. Sex wasn't important to him, although he'd never had trouble functioning. What interested him more was The Game. And part of The Game involved the buildup. And that took time.

But for Fab the attraction was a complex mosaic, and Lawrence quickly learned to play off every motif. He made sure they liked the same clubs, shared a taste for similar movies, and for hairy, good-looking men, which worked out well for maintaining a trouble-free friendship. Every once in a while, Fab made noises about fucking him, and Lawrence passed it off as a joke. Then, later, a pointed remark to Fab, that sex between them was out of the question, wasn't it? That the relationship would never go beyond friendship.... Then, when Fab seemed distressed enough, resigned, then the come on. A subtle touch here, a comment there. All of it designed to rev Fab up again. And then the questions, prying into Lawrence's fabricated past, the hints, finally the blatant offers, then the rejection. It had been a good Game, going around and around to Lawrence's delight, and had lasted longer than most. But he was tired of it.

They climbed the icy steps to the second floor non-descript door. Inside, they hiked the steep, narrow staircase to the third floor. Fab unlocked his door and they entered black space.

"Forget to pay your electric bill?" Lawrence asked. But when the lights didn't come on, he fumbled inside his jacket pocket for a lighter.

As the flame came to life, Fab walked around the room striking matches and lighting candles; there were many dozens.

"When did you get into hot wax?" Lawrence asked, but Fab didn't reply. It suddenly seemed pressing to Lawrence to know what Fab did for a living, how he spent his time when they weren't together. That, he suddenly realized, was foolish thinking, and he dismissed such useless thoughts. Better to know nothing about them. It was easier that way.

The candlelight lit the living room in a way that cast shadows everywhere, although Lawrence's own was not visible, which made him feel even more alien than he normally felt. The large space, as with so many Montreal apartments, had a kitchen off one end, and a bedroom off the other.

Lawrence walked around, gazing at everything as if this were a museum. Religious paraphernalia abounded, icons from a variety of faiths, and even a display of hands with blood prints on the palms.

Vampires were the main theme, though, in all shapes, sizes, colors and materials. Bela faces, photographs of Christopher Lee and Gary Oldman, statues of anonymous Draculas, dolls with capes and fangs, all either dangling from the walls and ceilings, or perched on shelves, or hovering menacingly in corners, or carved into the wooden arms of the sofa and poised on the table tops. Besides the obvious theme, another commonality became clear: each face was hideous in its lust and starvation; the overall effect was cheap and tawdry. It made Lawrence feel superior to this tasteless man.

"You've been dying to come here," Fab said, which caused Lawrence to laugh slightly. "So now that you're here, you might as well get comfy."

Fab's voice had turned serious, more serious than Lawrence was accustomed to hearing it, and he wondered if pushing this was a bad idea. He wasn't afraid, just surprised, but he didn't want any complications, especially heavy emotional scenes, now that The Game had come to the end. Fab was so shallow, always up, always lifting the half-full beer glass for inspection. For a while, Lawrence had found the contrast between his own somber nature and Fab's lively of-the-people temperament intriguing; now it just irritated him. Fab was boring. But like so many of the lower-class, he was also prone to melodrama; the vampire-covered walls between this apartment and the next were paper thin.

Lawrence took a seat on a *Louis Quatorze* chaise, covered in what might have been cheap blood-red velvet. Appropriate, Lawrence thought. "Aren't you going to sit?" he asked Fab. But Fab continued standing in front of him.

"Tell me, Larry, have you always been so dismal?"

Lawrence hated being called Larry, and Fab knew that. But he wasn't going to show it. "You should know me by now." Which, of course, was absurd; Fab didn't know him, would never know him.

"I know you, baby. I've known a lot of men like you."

"Oh please! This isn't going to be the List of Conquests, is it?"

"Not at all. I have nothing to prove. But you do."

Fab seemed to tower above him, confronting him in some way. Lawrence shifted uneasily. He had wanted to enjoy this, drag it out a bit, something to remember later. Maybe fast and furious was better this time. Maybe not. "Opting for melodrama?

"Listen, what do you have to drink?"

"Why? You never have more than a glass of wine a night. Or eat, that I've seen."

"The little man is observant."

"I've watched you. You just nudge the food around on your plate, and leave beverages sitting there all night—"

"Well, we all want Céline Dion's figure."

"Life doesn't interest you. Been there, done that. You're bored by existence and suck the life out of everybody you come in contact with because you're afraid to die."

Lawrence didn't know what to say. He had been bored a long long time. But that didn't give Fab the right to fracture his reality. Besides, this was his Game, his rules. "It's not my fault if people are vulgar and deadly dull. Even the lowest creature with sensibilities crawling on this planet would be jaded."

"I'm not."

"You've just proved my point, darling! Give it a rest."

"Watched *The Boys in the Band* one too many times, Larry? You're a walking cliché. Maybe it's time to use the stake on you, move you on, leave a space for others who might find life fascinating."

"Others? You mean, like you? Give me a break! You wallow in everything that's pedestrian, and call it intriguing. You have about as much style as some two-point-five daddy in the burbs!"

How did it get to this? Lawrence wondered. This cusp of intensity. Fab was close to yanking feelings out of him—angry feelings—long buried. God only knew what was behind them! They had never been friends, but they were becoming enemies, and that would not do. And suddenly the familiar non-feeling washed over him; he just didn't care. If they argued. If they didn't. He would never see Fab again after this night. Even the knowledge of that left him on the pleasant side of comfortably flat.

Suddenly, Fab dropped to his knees, taking Lawrence totally by surprise. He crawled forward, pressing between Lawrence's legs. Candlelight flickered on his handsome features; he resembled a supplicant in this room full of the relics of faith and faithlessness. His fingers found the belt, unbuckled it, pulled down the zipper, eased down the jeans.

In the darkness, Lawrence smirked. This is how it always went: They wanted it. No, they needed it. And that sealed their doom. Tomorrow Lawrence would be gone, leaving an empty shell behind.

But they were all cast from the same mold, these bubble boys. They never 'fessed up to what they really were about, to be used and abused in ways they couldn't even envision. To be hurt to the core, and left wounded, bleeding to death. That's what turns them on. The ultimate passion, the thing that takes them to the edge and then shoves them over, where they're terrified to go but are nevertheless headed. And Lawrence was the one to take them there. His inhuman coolness attracted them. And these pathetic beings thought he was just struggling to open up!

Fab had Lawrence's cock in his mouth and was working it with emotion, like there would be no tomorrow. And for him, there wouldn't be. The thick lips kissed and sucked lovingly, enthusiastically, just the way Fab did everything. Lawrence felt the pressure in his balls. What Fab would drink would seal his fate. He could not envision such chilling semen. Just as none of the ones before him had been able to envision it either.

Lawrence's only regret, if he had a regret, was that he was never around to see them the next day, devastated, the victims of a callous killer, who nourished himself on souls, not food, and who consumed essence instead of fine wine.

He lay his head back against the chaise. Above, a caped, corpse-like form extended from the wall and leered down at him in the candlelight. The creature was from another realm, a dark and lonely place that he knew so well, that was all he knew. Lawrence stared into its stone-cold eyes as Fab made the frigid juices burst from his cock. And then Lawrence screamed, as he always did when they finally took it from him. The semen pumped until there was nothing more to offer at this alter of vapid existence. Until he was completely drained, and needed replenishing.

It was time to end this, to bring it to its natural conclusion. Lawrence gripped the arm of the chaise hard, and struggled to his feet. The darkness of this candle-lit crypt Fab called home bothered him. And he felt unbearably weak. Oddly, his cock still throbbed. He needed to act fast, before his energy gave out and time did him in.

Fab stood too. His face seemed filled out, as if the cold beverage he had extracted from Lawrence had nourished him. Even his lips were dark in the dim light, and his eyes glittered with life. "Poor puppy," he said, as if he were old and Lawrence just a boy. "You just don't understand life, do you? How important it is to live it."

The room spun. Lawrence sank to his knees hitting something hard, like packed earth. Images flew past his swirling vision, creatures of the darkness come to life to carry him through the door to their realm—had he so long slept on the doorsteps, awaiting entrance?

Blood rushed from his head. How had Fab drained him? And then he knew. The face there, hovering, so full and alive, bloated, lived off *everything* in its path, indiscriminately. The full, the empty; the successful, the failures; the living and the dead. He embraced all equally, ravishing, continually nourishing himself. Lawrence was a novice player compared to this one, and he suddenly understood with shocking clarity that this time he had gone about The Game all wrong.

"My blood..." he managed, feeling the wet stickiness between his legs, wondering if the words had even left his lips.

They must have, because Fab answered, "Tasty. Refined. Definitely one of the special ones, Larry. But you know, it all ends up in the same place, mixed in here with the rest."

Focusing on Fab's face in the near darkness was nearly impossible. But his eyes said it all. Darkness that fed off darkness and light and expanded, eternally. And what the eyes expressed so eloquently, the two sharp incisors said in a more blatant way: Lawrence was nothing special. Nothing at all.

Against his will, Lawrence's eyelids dropped. His heartbeat slowed. He watched himself pitch forward into a widening chasm. Down below, he saw the blood-pool of humanity rise up to embrace him. What he had consumed, he had become. The blood drowned his screams, but not Fab's laughter.

𝕭𝖊𝖑𝖆 𝕷𝖚𝖌𝖔𝖘𝖎 𝕴𝖘 𝕯𝖊𝖆𝖉

RON OLIVER

Me and David were vampires.

I'm saying "were" because it's been like six years since I saw him in person and you never know how time changes people, especially with all these weird diseases and shit going around now. All I really know is that he got married and lives somewhere up in Colorado, and the only reason I even know that much is because I found his mother out in Santa Cruz and after a little convincing she told me everything. Actually, it was a lot of convincing but it wasn't my fault, she pissed me off.

What're you gonna do?

Me and David met at Beverly Hills High on September the fifth, nineteen eighty-six. Or seven. Things get sort of blurry for me about dates and shit, but I guess it doesn't really matter when anyway, just that we met. Eleventh grade homeroom and I'm sitting in my usual desk, which is the sixth from the front, sixth from the left and sixth from the back. Six six six, get it?

So I'm sitting there using the sharp point on the end of the compass from my geometry set to kind of burrow some holes on the inside of my arm just down from the Ministry tattoo I did myself after my fucking mother's accountant canceled my fucking credit card thank you very fucking much. And I'm licking up the blood but secretly, hiding down behind a physics book I've got propped up in front of me, when Mr. Heim the geek teacher says,

"Alright people, face front. This is David Grant—"

and I'm telling you it was like looking in a fucking mirror. This guy is standing there, my exact size, same brown hair hanging almost to his shoulders, same kind of black T-shirt (except his was Morrisey and mine was Bauhaus), same kind of silver bracelets, and almost the exact same earring: a hoop with a skull hanging from his left ear. He was even wearing the same black 501's, and I'm not a faggot or anything, but they were so tight you could see his dick and balls making a really obvious bulge high up on his left thigh. Just like mine.

"—Just transferred here from San Diego. Let's all give him a hearty Beverly High welcome."

So Heim starts clapping and then the rest of the class joins in like fucking chimpanzees and this guy, David, he doesn't so much walk as *glide* to an empty desk across from mine and slips into the seat. He kind of smirks at the rest of the dorks in the place and then looks over at me, probably because I was the only one not clapping. But instead of looking at my face, he looks at my chest, at my Bauhaus T-shirt with the cool picture from that movie *The Closet of Dr. Caligari* or whatever the fuck it's called, and then he looks down at the floor, at the drops of blood that have been falling from the holes in my arm all this time and then he looks right at me with his eyes, blue eyes the same color as those thick veins that rope up your arms when you're holding on to something really tight, and he smiles and that's when I knew we were going to be friends.

Me and David ditched a lot that year. Mostly we'd just check in at homeroom and then get the fuck out of there and go to his place, or mine usually since my mother was on location a lot that year making two of those stupid fucking *Police School* movies back to back. We'd smoke some rad Mexicali cheeb I bought off our gardener and watch horror movies on the big screen TV my dad gave me the day the divorce went through. None of that stupid fucking classic stuff either, that old black and white Bela Lugosi-in-a-cape-shit. We did *Evil Dead, Texas Chainsaw*, some Italian zombie junk. We tried to get through *I Spit on Your Grave* but it was total crap, except for the part where the chick cuts off the guy's dick. David thought that was hilarious. I liked the blood spurting up from between his legs and the sort of dumbass look on his face like "Uh, what happened to my dick?"

So, anyway, the vampire thing. It kind of happened by accident, I guess. I mean, just because you dress in black and listen to cool music and wear eyeliner and stay out of the sun doesn't mean you're the Undead, right? You might just be one of those old guys from the Rolling Stones. And for me and David, it was more like a private club, you know, no girls allowed. At least, that's how it started. That, and *The Hunger*.

We must have seen that movie like two hundred times, especially the part where the chick from *Rocky Horror Picture Show* and that French babe get it on. I didn't really get off on it, but David'd just sit there with his eyes all hazy from the pot and watch it over and over, not saying anything, nothing at all. Until one day—it was a Thursday—I remember because we were supposed to be in gym, and after the French chick grunts like she's coming or something, David puts it on freeze frame so Janet's face is jiggling on the screen with blood all over her lips. And he kind of looks at me out of the corner of his eye and gets this funny smile on his face and says,
"You ever think about doing that?"
and I go,
"Uh. Yeah. Sure,"
and he goes,
"You wanna try it?"
and I go,
"You mean right now? You and me?"
and he goes,
"I guess,"
and then he takes off his shirt. Which I'm thinking is kind of weird because you really only need to cut the neck or maybe the wrist to get a steady flow of blood. So I do the same and we both kind of look at each other for about a minute. He's thinner than me, with some little sprouts of hair just starting around his belly button and kind of trailing down under the band of his Mr. Briefs. He leans back on my bed and neither one of us says anything; we're just breathing and looking at each other, waiting to see who goes first.

So I get up and walk over to my new Bang and Olufson CD player, the one my dad sent from London because he forgot to call me on my birthday, and put in Siouxsie and the Banshees and by the time I press play and turn around, David is sitting on my bed totally bare-assed, his jeans and underpants turned inside out on the floor. I don't know what to say so I just go,
"Wow,"
and then he goes,
"Let's go,"
and I walk across the room to the bed. When I get there, I can see his dick hanging down between his legs, and he watches me looking at it but doesn't say anything, he just keeps looking at me and it's

making me feel kind of weird so I take off the rest of my clothes and then we're even.

"You go first,"

he says and closes his eyes. The room is kind of cold and my dick is starting to shrivel up into my crotch so I think *well this is it* and then I reach over to my desk and find my old Boy Scout knife, the one I got from Uncle Ted for never telling, and it makes a noise when I open it but David doesn't open his eyes and then I lift it up and for a second I can see my reflection in the blade and suddenly I'm not sixteen, I'm sixteen hundred and my name is Vlad and my skin is the color of a statue in a museum and its name is David and he is spread out beneath me and then I push the knife against my forearm until I hear the little "pop" of the skin giving way and feel the cold metal and I slide the silver edge all along my arm until the blood starts to drip and traces a line along David's thighs and past his cock and stomach and nipples and up to his lips and he opens his eyes and he looks surprised and then he closes his mouth.

Which is the stupidest fucking thing because now my blood is dribbling down on his face and neck and he's just wasting it. So I go,

"What the fuck are you doing?"

but instead of answering he reaches up and wraps his hand around my neck and pulls me down closer to him, until our faces are so close I can feel his hot breath drying out my contact lenses and then he says,

"Suck me,"

and starts pushing on my head, smearing my face in the blood on his neck. And I think *yeah, okay, whatever* and I open my mouth and try to get my teeth on his throat but the blood is so slippery I can't get a good bite and David's not helping at all because he just keeps pushing me lower and lower. Down his chest, bumping along his ribs, rubbing past his blood soaked bush, he keeps shoving until something hard slaps against my cheek. And even though I already know what it is, it's still a surprise to see how long and hard his dick really is, curving up toward me, the slit on the end gaping open like a mouth or something. And he goes,

"Suck me, man,"

again, in kind of a whisper, and I'm lying there with my blood smeared all over my face and chest and his body, with his stiff wood like three inches from my mouth and it's covered in blood too, and Siouxsie's singing

Peekaaabooo
Peekaaabooo

and you know how hard-ons are sort of like contagious, so when I look down at my own dick it's sticking straight up and just throbbing like a fucking toothache and you know as well as I do that it's throbbing because of one thing and one thing only and that one thing is blood.

So I close my eyes and open my mouth.

At first all I taste is the same old metal of my own blood, but then after he pushes and pushes and I almost gag like twice there's suddenly another taste, warm and salty, and I think *wow, he's really bleeding a lot* but then I remember what it is and I'm kind of surprised that I like it, because I know we're not faggots, neither one of us, and that's when I realize what I should've known all along, the thing that explains everything.

Me and David are vampires.

So anyway, what I want to tell you is after that we spent every day together and we never went to school and we never went to the mall and we never did anything except be vampires in my room.

But that'd be bullshit because that's not what happened at all. What really happened is that everything between me and David went to shit. What really *really* happened was Sarah.

Sarah with an H she'd say like it was some stupid fucking secret code that only she and David knew about and then she'd laugh and it sounded like breaking glass and she smelled like fresh laundry just out of the dryer only somebody'd put in too many of those little blue sheets and it'd almost make you want to puke.

After that first time with David, things changed really fast. He didn't want to ditch class anymore and he started acting like we weren't friends, just guys who said hi in the hall at school. And then one day he showed up wearing a blue sweater with a white T-shirt underneath it. Blue. And white. Color.

Something was wrong.

So one day after gym class, while the rest of the stupid fucking geeks were changing out of their stinking jocks and T-shirts and into their Gap jeans and button-down collar fucking shirts, I got David alone in the shower. He wasn't looking at me, he had his eyes closed letting the hot water splash down over his body and I just stood there for like about a minute and looked at him, shining in the steam, and then I go,

"So what've you been doing?"

and he opens his eyes suddenly, like he's surprised to see me there and maybe a little bit scared because he looks around to see if anybody else is in the shower and then he goes,

"Nothing,"

and just goes back to showering like I'm not even there so I go,

"I got tickets to that Echo concert on Sunday,"

and he goes,

"Mmm hmm,"

so I go,

"You wanna go with me?"

and he goes,

"Can't. Gotta work,"

which was news to me because I didn't even know he had a fucking job, but I didn't want him to think I gave a fuck so I just go,

"Whatever,"

and then I leave with my towel in front of me because I'm starting to get a hard-on just being that close to him, which is totally fucked I guess but sometimes you can't help it, right?

That night after dinner, which the stupid fucking maid burnt anyway, I watched *The Hunger* again, trying to find that exact place where David freeze-framed but I kept missing it. Mostly because my stupid fucking remote-control batteries died, but also I guess because the smoke was pretty thick in my room from those Echo tickets burning in my garbage can.

Which you probably think is pretty fucking stupid, me burning perfectly good concert tickets just because some guy has to work, but see I didn't just stay home that night. No, the night of the Echo concert I went down to the Tower Records store, you know the big one on Sunset, and I looked around for awhile. Except I wasn't really looking for CDs or anything, I was looking for David because that's where his mom said he was working, only some skinny guy with greasy hair and a bandage on his nose goes,

"David's not working tonight,"

and I go,
"He said he was,"
and the skinny guy goes,
"I think he and Sarah went to the movies,"
and then those shitty lights in that place got really bright and all
I could hear was the stupid fucking Beatles singing "Hey Jude" and
it made me think that maybe there should have been three more
Mark David Chapmans and I pushed the skinny guy against a rack
of U2 discs and he goes,
"Hey,"
but I don't even bother to look at him I just get the fuck out of
the store and into the blue BMW my father gave me because he
wanted to be with his new kids for Christmas this year and he hoped
I understood and I crank up The Cure and play "Disintegration"
over and over again until I get to David's just in time to see him
walking a girl I've seen in my geometry class out to a white Cabriolet
and they're holding hands and they kiss before she gets into the car
and drives away and he just stands there watching her go and then
goes back into his house and I have to burn three craters on the
inside of my arm with my car lighter before I stop crying.

Two days later, the maid's day off, and Sarah is standing at my
front door, smiling, her geometry books under her arm and she
goes,
"You have no idea how great this is. I really need the money,"
and I go,
"And I really need to pass geometry."
I smile, being careful that she doesn't see all my teeth, and she
walks into my house and I take one look out at the empty street and
her Cabriolet parked in the driveway and then I close the door.

The phone rings like five times before David goes,
"Hello,"
and I go,
"Hey,"
and he goes,
"Uh. Hey,"
and then I don't say anything, I just kind of let it go real quiet and
then he goes,

"Um. What?"
and I laugh a bit and go,
"You wanna come over for awhile?"
and he goes,
"Nah, I gotta—"
but I don't let him finish before I go,
"Sarah's here,"
and he goes,
"What?"
and I hang up.

When my mother's new boyfriend Karl asked me to do those pictures for him, the ones you probably heard about or maybe you saw them in that magazine before they took it off the shelves, he gave me this really cool Swiss Army watch that keeps totally perfect time so I know it takes exactly twelve minutes and twenty-three seconds before David comes through the front door and goes,
"Sarah?"
with this sort of freaked voice that makes me laugh a bit and I go,
"In here,"
and he runs in wearing jeans and a jacket with no shirt and cowboy boots and he starts to say something but then stops like completely dead and just stands there and I'm not really sure what surprises him the most.

Maybe it's the bootleg Ministry CD blasting at eleven or the sixty-six six-inch candles burning all over the living room or me standing there like totally naked with a hard-on and covered in blood or the cool plastic and rubber fangs in my mouth that I stole from the makeup trailer on my mother's new movie *Daughter of Death*.

Or maybe it's that he sees the big metal and stone coffee table propped up on one end with two Westside phone books, tilted at just the right angle so that the blood from the two geometry compass holes I cut in Sarah's neck trickles down to the wide glass ashtray I gave my parents on their twelfth anniversary because he goes,
"Fuck Fuck Fuck."

Her eyes are blinking but I guess she's in a coma or something because she's stopped crying and pulling on the black electric tape and even though she's naked she's not shivering anymore.

Me and David look at each other and he goes,

"You're fucked,"
and I start to go,
"Yeah, whatever,"
but he fucking jumps me and starts punching me in the mouth.
He shatters the fangs into pieces and I have to spit them out before
I fucking choke to death and then we're rolling on the floor and
smearing Sarah-with-an-H's blood all over our bodies and then he's
sitting on top of me with his knees clamped so tight around my
chest I can hardly breathe and he's punching me in the face again
and again and I start to get dizzy and I'm not sure if it's from him
hitting me or if it's from me swallowing so much of Sarah's blood
and my arms are flapping around like I'm drowning or something
and then my hand grabs the ceramic seahorse that some guy my
mother fucked last summer gave her as a good-bye gift and I smash
it into the side of David's head.

He drops to the floor with a grunt and a cut over his eye that's
already starting to bleed and for a second I think about holding him
down to lick the wound but then he wipes it with the back of his
hand and curls his lip like he's tasting shit and he goes,
"You fucking killed her you fucking killed her,"
and I go,
"No,"
and I get up and sort of stagger over to the coffee table, still bare-
assed but my hard-on's gone and my dick just sort of bobs along
with me as I pick up one of the pearl-handled steak knives I won
last Halloween because a guy at Knott's Berry Farm couldn't guess
my weight and I go,
"We can bring her back,"
and I hold out the knife toward David. He backs away a little bit
like he's afraid I'm going to stab him and I almost laugh but it's hard
because my mouth is swelling up from where he punched me so I
go,
"She's for you, man. I brought her here for you. She'll be yours
forever,"
and I turn the handle toward him and go,
"Your blood. Like the movie,"
and his eyes open wider, like he's starting to get it and I go,
"Give her your blood."
I suddenly get this really fucking sick smell coming from David

and I look down and see that he's pissed his pants and that almost makes me laugh again and then I see that he's crying, really hard, like a little kid and the tears are cutting white lines through the blood smeared across his cheeks and he just goes,

"No no no no no,"

and I figure that he's not in the mood to handle it right now so I walk back around the table and hold my left arm, the one with the Ministry tattoo, up over Sarah's body and use the knife to cut my wrist wide open and I shove it against her lips, the blood spraying from the gash into her mouth and I go,

"Drink from me and live forever,"

except she either doesn't hear me or else she doesn't want eternal life because she doesn't swallow, she just lets the blood trickle out of her mouth, some of it splashing across her cheeks and some of it running in thin rivers down into her open eyes so I go,

"Drink! Drink you stupid fucking bitch,"

and I can hear David crying louder now and the room starts flashing red and at first I think it's the blood but then I hear the sirens and realize Sarah doesn't want to be a vampire after all.

Me and David didn't see each other after that. He and his family moved away and you probably know what happened to me.

But it's funny you know, how things are. Like I said before, I haven't seen David in person for six years, as long as I was in State. Still that doesn't mean we haven't spoken.

I told you me and David are vampires. Every night I was in that place, after the last light was turned out, after the last crazy was strapped into bed, after the last needle was shoved into a vein, he would talk to me. Well, okay, not exactly to me. But the cockroaches, the flies, even the occasional rat, they all brought me messages.

From him.

And that's why I'm driving now. And it's why I tore the hospital guard's eyes out with my teeth and dressed in his uniform and stole his car. And why I spent almost two hours shoving David's mother's hand down her kitchen garbage disposal to get his address. And why nothing's going to stop me between here and Colorado.

Me and David are vampires. And he sent me a message begging me to come and meet his wife.

And his baby.

Yum.

His Mouth Will Taste of Wormwood

POPPY Z. BRITE

"To the treasures and the pleasures of the grave," said my friend Louis, and raised his goblet of absinthe to me in drunken benediction.

"To the funeral lilies," I replied, "and to the calm pale bones." I drank deeply from my own glass. The absinthe cauterized my throat with its flavor, part pepper, part licorice, part rot. It had been one of our greatest finds: more than fifty bottles of the now-outlawed liqueur, sealed up in a New Orleans family tomb. Transporting them was a nuisance, but once we had learned to enjoy the taste of wormwood, our continued drunkenness was ensured for a long, long time. We had taken the skull of the crypt's patriarch, too, and it now resided in a velvet-lined enclave in our museum.

Louis and I, you see, were dreamers of a dark and restless sort. We met in our second year of college and quickly found that we shared one vital trait: both of us were dissatisfied with everything. We drank straight whiskey and declared it too weak. We took strange drugs, but the visions they brought us were of emptiness, mindlessness, slow decay. The books we read were dull; the artists who sold their colorful drawings on the street were mere hacks in our eyes; the music we heard was never loud enough, never harsh enough to stir us. We were truly jaded, we told one another. For all the impression the world made upon us, our eyes might have been dead black holes in our heads.

For a time we thought our salvation lay in the sorcery wrought by music. We studied recordings of weird nameless dissonances, attended performances of obscure bands at ill-lit filthy clubs. But music did not save us. For a time we distracted ourselves with carnality. We explored the damp alien territory between the legs of any girl who would have us, sometimes separately, sometimes both of us in bed together with one girl or more. We bound their wrists and ankles with black lace, we lubricated and penetrated their every orifice, we shamed them with their own pleasures. I recall a mauve-haired beauty, Felicia, who was brought to wild sobbing orgasm by the rough tongue of a stray dog we trapped. We watched her from across the room, drug-dazed and unstirred.

When we had exhausted the possibilities of women, we sought those of our own sex, craving the androgynous curve of a boy's cheekbone, the molten flood of ejaculation invading our mouths. Eventually we turned to one another, seeking the thresholds of pain and ecstasy no one else had been able to help us attain. Louis asked me to grow my nails long and file them into needle-sharp points. When I raked them down his back, tiny beads of blood welled up in the angry tracks they left. He loved to lie still, pretending to submit to me, as I licked the salty blood away. Afterward he would push me down and attack me with his mouth, his tongue seeming to sear a trail of liquid fire into my skin.

But sex did not save us either. We shut ourselves in our room and saw no one for days on end. At last we withdrew to the seclusion of Louis's ancestral home near Baton Rouge. Both his parents were dead—a suicide pact, Louis hinted, or perhaps a suicide and a murder. Louis, the only child, retained the family home and fortune. Built on the edge of a vast swamp, the plantation house loomed sepulchrally out of the gloom that surrounded it always, even in the middle of a summer afternoon. Oaks of primordial hugeness grew in a canopy over the house, their branches like black arms fraught with Spanish moss. The moss was everywhere, reminding me of brittle gray hair, stirring wraithlike in the dank breeze from the swamp. I had the impression that, left too long unchecked, the moss might begin to grow from the ornate window-frames and fluted columns of the house itself.

The place was deserted save for us. The air was heady with the luminous scent of magnolias and the fetor of swamp gas. At night we sat on the veranda and sipped bottles of wine from the family cellar, gazing through an increasingly alcoholic mist at the will-o'-the-wisps that beckoned far off in the swamp. Obsessively we talked of new thrills and how we might get them. Louis's wit sparkled liveliest when he was bored, and on the night he first mentioned grave robbing, I laughed. I could not imagine that he was serious.

"What would we do with a bunch of dried-up old remains? Grind them to make a voodoo potion? I preferred your idea of increasing our tolerance to various poisons."

Louis's sharp face snapped toward me. His eyes were painfully sensitive to light, so that even in this gloaming he wore tinted glasses and it was impossible to see his expression. He kept his fair hair clipped very short, so that it stood up in crazy tufts when he raked a nervous hand through it. "No, Howard. Think of it: our own collection of death. A catalogue of pain, of human frailty—all for us. Set against a backdrop of tranquil loveliness. Think what it would be to walk through such a place, meditating, reflecting upon your own ephemeral essence. Think of making love in a charnel-house! We have only to assemble the parts—they will create a whole into which we may fall."

(Louis enjoyed speaking in cryptic puns; anagrams and palindromes, too, and any sort of puzzle appealed to him. I wonder whether that was not the root of his determination to look into the fathomless eye of death and master it. Perhaps he saw the mortality of the flesh as a gigantic jigsaw or crossword which, if he fitted all the parts into place, he might solve and thus defeat. Louis would have loved to live forever, though he would never have known what to do with all his time.)

He soon produced his hashish pipe to sweeten the taste of the wine, and we spoke no more of grave robbing that night. But the thought preyed upon me in the languorous weeks to come. The smell of a freshly opened grave, I thought, must in its way be as intoxicating as the perfume of the swamp or a girl's most intimate sweat. Could we truly assemble a collection of the grave's treasures that would be lovely to look upon, that would soothe our fevered souls?

The caresses of Louis's tongue grew languid. Sometimes, instead of nestling with me between the black satin sheets of our bed, he would sleep on a torn blanket in one of the underground rooms. These had originally been built for indeterminate but always intriguing purposes—abolitionist meetings had taken place there, Louis told me, and a weekend of free love, and an earnest but wildly incompetent Black Mass replete with a vestal virgin and phallic candles.

These rooms were where our museum would be set up. At last I came to agree with Louis that only the plundering of graves might cure us of the most stifling ennui we had yet suffered. I could not bear to watch his tormented sleep, the pallor of his hollow cheeks, the delicate bruise-like darkening of the skin beneath his flickering eyes. Besides, the notion of grave robbing had begun to entice me.

In ultimate corruption, might we not find the path to ultimate salvation?

Our first grisly prize was the head of Louis's mother, rotten as a pumpkin forgotten on the vine, half-shattered by two bullets from an antique Civil War revolver. We took it from the family crypt by the light of a full moon. The will-o'-the-wisps glowed weakly, like dying beacons on some unattainable shore, as we crept back to the manse. I dragged pick and shovel behind me; Louis carried the putrescent trophy tucked beneath his arm. After we had descended into the museum, I lit three candles scented with the russet spices of autumn (the season when Louis's parents had died) while Louis placed the head in the alcove we had prepared for it. I thought I detected a certain tenderness in his manner. "May she give us the family blessing," he murmured, absently wiping on the lapel of his jacket a few shreds of pulpy flesh that had adhered to his fingers.

We spent a happy time refurbishing the museum, polishing the inlaid precious metals of the wall fixtures, brushing away the dust that frosted the velvet designs of the wallpaper, alternately burning incense and charring bits of cloth we had saturated with our blood, in order to give the rooms the odor we desired—a charnel perfume strong enough to drive us to frenzy. We travelled far in our collections, but always we returned home with crates full of things no man had ever been meant to possess. We heard of a girl with violet eyes who had died in some distant town; not seven days later we had those eyes in an ornate cut-glass jar, pickled in formaldehyde. We scraped bone dust and nitre from the bottoms of ancient coffins; we stole the barely withered heads and hands of children fresh in their graves, with their soft little fingers and their lips like flower petals. We had baubles and precious heirlooms, vermiculated prayer-books and shrouds encrusted with mold. I had not taken seriously Louis's talk of making love in a charnel-house—but neither had I reckoned on the pleasure he could inflict with a femur dipped in rose-scented oil.

Upon the night I speak of—the night we drank our toast to the grave and its riches—we had just acquired our finest prize yet. Later in the evening we planned a celebratory debauch at a nightclub in the city. We had returned from our most recent travels not with the usual assortment of sacks and crates, but with only one small box carefully wrapped and tucked into Louis's breast pocket. The box contained an object whose existence we had only speculated upon previously. From certain half-articulate mutterings of an old blind man plied with cheap liquor in a French Quarter bar, we traced rumors of a certain fetish or charm to a Negro graveyard in the southern bayou country. The fetish was said to be a thing of eerie beauty, capable of luring any lover to one's bed, hexing any enemy to a sick and painful death, and (this, I think, was what intrigued Louis the most) turning back tenfold on anyone who used it with less than the touch of a master.

A heavy mist hung low over the graveyard when we arrived there, lapping at our ankles, pooling around the markers of wood and stone, abruptly melting away in patches to reveal a gnarled root or a patch of blackened grass, then closing back in. By the light of a waning moon we made our way along a path overgrown with rioting weeds. The graves were decorated with elaborate mosaics of broken glass, coins, bottlecaps, oyster shells lacquered silver and gold. Some mounds were outlined by empty bottles shoved neck-downward into the earth. I saw a lone plaster saint whose features had been worn away by years of wind and rain. I kicked half-buried rusty cans that had once held flowers; now they held only bare brittle stems and pestilent rainwater, or nothing at all. Only the scent of wild spider lilies pervaded the night.

The earth in one corner of the graveyard seemed blacker than the rest. The grave we sought was marked only by a crude cross of charred and twisted wood. We were skilled at the art of violating the dead; soon we had the coffin uncovered. The boards were warped by years of burial in wet, foul earth. Louis pried up the lid with his spade and, by the moon's meager and watery light, we gazed upon what lay within.

Of the inhabitant we knew almost nothing. Some said a hideously disfigured old conjure woman lay buried here. Some said she was a young girl with a face as lovely and cold as moonlight on water, and a soul crueler than Fate itself. Some claimed the body was not a woman's at all, but that of a white voodoo priest who had ruled the bayou. He had features of a cool, unearthly beauty, they said, and a stock of fetishes and potions which he would hand out with the kindest blessing...or the direst curse. This was the story Louis and I liked best; the sorcerer's capriciousness appealed to us, and the fact that he was beautiful.

No trace of beauty remained to the thing in the coffin—at least not the sort of beauty that a healthy eye might cherish. Louis and I loved the translucent parchment skin stretched tight over long bones that seemed to have been carved from ivory. The delicate brittle hands folded across the sunken chest, the soft black caverns of the eyes, the colorless strands of hair that still clung to the fine white dome of the skull—to us these things were the poetry of death.

Louis played his flashlight over the withered cords of the neck. There, on a silver chain gone black with age, was the object we had come seeking. No crude wax doll or bit of dried root was this. Louis and I gazed at each other, moved by the beauty of the thing; then, as if in a dream, he reached to grasp it. This was our rightful night's prize, our plunder from a sorcerer's grave.

"How does it look?" Louis asked as we were dressing.

I never had to think about my clothes. On an evening such as this, when we were dressing to go out, I would choose the same garments I might wear for a night's digging in the graveyard—black, unornamented black, with only the whiteness of my face and hands showing against the backdrop of night. On a particularly festive occasion, such as this, I might smudge a bit of kohl round my eyes. The absence of color made me nearly invisible: if I walked with my shoulders hunched and my chin tucked down, no one except Louis would see me.

"Don't slouch so, Howard," said Louis irritably as I ducked past the mirror. "Turn around and look at me. Aren't I fine in my sorcerer's jewelry?"

Even when Louis wore black, he did it to be noticed. Tonight he was resplendent in narrow-legged trousers of purple paisley silk and a silvery jacket that seemed to turn all light iridescent. He had taken our prize out of its box and fastened it around his throat. As I came closer to look at it, I caught Louis's scent: rich and rather meaty, like blood kept too long in a stoppered bottle.

Against the sculpted hollow of Louis's throat, the thing on its chain seemed more strangely beautiful than ever. Have I neglected to describe the magical object, the voodoo fetish from the churned earth of the grave? I will never forget it. A polished sliver of bone (or a tooth, but what fang could have been so long, so sleekly honed, and still have somehow retained the look of a *human tooth?*) bound by a strip of copper. Set into the metal, a single ruby sparkled like a drop of gore against the verdigris. Etched in exquisite miniature upon the sliver of bone, and darkened by the rubbing in of some black-red substance, was an elaborate vévé—one of the symbols used by voodooists to invoke their pantheon of terrible gods. Whoever was buried in that lonely bayou grave, he had been no mere dabbler in swamp magic. Every cross and swirl of the vévé was reproduced to perfection. I thought the thing still retained a trace of the grave's scent—a dark odor like potatoes long spoiled. Each grave has its own peculiar scent, just as each living body does.

"Are you certain you should wear it?" I asked.

"It will go into the museum tomorrow," he said, "with a scarlet candle burning eternally before it. Tonight its powers are mine."

The nightclub was in a part of the city that looked as if it had been gutted from the inside out by a righteous tongue of fire. The street was lit only by occasional scribbles of neon high overhead, advertisements for cheap hotels and all-night bars. Dark eyes stared at us from the crevices and pathways between buildings, disappearing only when Louis's hand crept toward the inner pocket of his jacket. He carried a small stiletto there, and knew how to use it for more than pleasure.

We slipped through a door at the end of an alley and descended the narrow staircase into the club. The lurid glow of a blue bulb flooded the stairs, making Louis's face look sunken and dead behind his tinted glasses. Feedback blasted us as we came in, and above it, a screaming battle of guitars. The inside of the club was a patchwork of flickering light and darkness. Graffiti covered the walls and the ceiling like a tangle of barbed wire come alive. I saw bands' insignia and jeering death's-heads, crucifixes bejewelled with broken glass and black obscenities writhing in the stroboscopic light.

Louis brought me a drink from the bar. I sipped it slowly, still drunk on absinthe. Since the music was too loud for conversation, I studied the clubgoers around us. A quiet bunch, they were, staring fixedly at the stage as if they had been drugged (and no doubt many of them had—I remembered visiting a club one night on a dose of hallucinogenic mushrooms, watching in fascination as the guitar strings seemed to drip soft viscera onto the stage). Younger than Louis and myself, most of them were, and queerly beautiful in their thrift-shop rags, their leather and fishnet and cheap costume jewelry, their pale faces and painted hair. Perhaps we would take one of them home with us tonight. We had done so before. "The delicious guttersnipes," Louis called them. A particularly beautiful face, starkly boned and androgynous, flickered at the edge of my vision. When I looked, it was gone.

I went into the restroom. A pair of boys stood at a single urinal, talking animatedly. I stood at the sink rinsing my hands, watching the boys in the mirror and trying to overhear their conversation. A hairline fracture in the glass seemed to pull the taller boy's eyes askew. "Caspar and Alyssa found her tonight," he said. "In some old warehouse by the river. I heard her skin was gray, man. And sort of withered, like something had sucked out most of the meat."

"Far out," said the other boy. His black-rimmed lips barely moved.

"She was only fifteen, you know?" said the tall boy as he zipped his ragged trousers.

"She was a cunt anyway."

They turned away from the urinal and started talking about the band—Ritual Sacrifice, I gathered, whose name was scrawled on the walls of the club. As they went out, the boys glanced at the mirror and the tall one's eyes met mine for an instant. Nose like a haughty Indian chief's, eyelids smudged with black and silver. Louis would approve, I thought—but the night was young, and there were many drinks left to be had.

When the band took a break we visited the bar again. Louis edged in beside a thin dark-haired boy who was bare-chested except for a piece of torn lace tied about his throat. When he turned, I knew his was the androgynous and striking face I had glimpsed before. His beauty was almost feral, but overlaid with a cool elegance like a veneer of sanity hiding madness. His ivory skin stretched over cheekbones like razors; his eyes were hectic pools of darkness.

"I like your amulet," he said to Louis. "It's very unusual."

"I have another one like it at home," Louis told him.

"Really? I'd like to see them both together." The boy paused to let Louis order our vodka gimlets, then said, "I thought there was only one."

Louis's back straightened like a string of beads being pulled taut. Behind his glasses, I knew, his pupils would have shrunk to pinpoints: the light pained him more when he was nervous. But no tremor in his voice betrayed him when he said, "What do you know about it?"

The boy shrugged. On his bony shoulders, the movement was insouciant and drop-dead graceful. "It's voodoo," he said. "I know what voodoo is. Do you?"

The implication stung, but Louis only bared his teeth the slightest bit; it might have been a smile. "I am *conversant* in all types of magic," he said, "at least."

The boy moved closer to Louis, so that their hips were almost touching, and lifted the amulet between thumb and forefinger. I thought I saw one long nail brush Louis's throat, but I could not be sure. "I could tell you the meaning of this vévé," he said, "if you were certain you wished to know."

"It symbolizes power," Louis said. "All the power of my soul." His voice was cold, but I saw his tongue dart out to moisten his lips. He was beginning to dislike this boy, and also to desire him.

"No," said the boy so softly that I barely caught his words. He sounded almost sad. "This cross in the center is inverted, you see, and the line encircling it represents a serpent. A thing like this can trap your soul. Instead of being rewarded with eternal life…you might be doomed to it."

"Doomed to eternal life?" Louis permitted himself a small cold smile. "Whatever do you mean?"

"The band is starting again. Find me after the show and I'll tell you. We can have a drink…and you can tell me all you know about voodoo." The boy threw back his head and laughed. Only then did I notice that one of his upper canine teeth was missing.

The next part of the evening remains a blur of moonlight and neon, ice cubes and blue swirling smoke and sweet drunkenness. The boy drank glass after glass of absinthe with us, seeming to relish the bitter taste. None of our other guests had liked the liqueur. "Where did you get it?" he asked. Louis was silent for a long moment before he said, "It was sent over from France." Except for its single black gap, the boy's smile would have been as perfect as the sharp-edged crescent moon.

"Another drink?" said Louis, refilling both our glasses.

When I next came to clarity, I was in the boy's arms. I could not make out the words he was whispering; they might have been an incantation, if magic may be sung to pleasure's music. A pair of hands cupped my face, guiding my lips over the boy's pale parchment skin. They might have been Louis's hands. I knew nothing except this boy, the fragile movement of the bones beneath the skin, the taste of his spit bitter with wormwood.

I do not remember when he finally turned away from me and began lavishing his love upon Louis. I wish I could have watched, could have seen the lust bleeding into Louis's eyes, the pleasure wracking his body. For, as it turned out, the boy loved Louis so much more thoroughly than ever he loved me.

When I awoke, the bass thump of my pulse echoing through my skull blotted out all other sensations. Gradually, though, I became aware of tangled silk sheets, of hot sunlight on my face. Not until I came fully awake did I see the thing I had cradled like a lover all through the night.

For an instant two realities shifted in uneasy juxtaposition and almost merged. I was in Louis's bed; I recognized the feel of the sheets, their odor of silk and sweat. But this thing I held—this was surely one of the fragile mummies we had dragged out of their graves, the things we dissected for our museum.

It took me only a moment, though, to recognize the familiar ruined features—the sharp chin, the high elegant brow. Something had desiccated Louis, had drained him of every drop of his moisture, his vitality. His skin crackled and flaked away beneath my fingers. His hair stuck to my lips, dry and colorless. The amulet, which had still been around his throat in bed last night, was gone.

The boy had left no trace—or so I thought until I saw a nearly transparent thing at the foot of the bed. It was like a quantity of spiderweb, or a damp and insubstantial veil. I picked it up and shook it out, but could not see its features until I held it up to the window. The thing was vaguely human-shaped, with empty limbs trailing off into nearly invisible tatters. As the thing wafted and billowed, I saw part of a face in it—the sharp curve left by a cheekbone, the hole where an eye had been—as if a face were imprinted upon gauze.

I carried Louis's brittle shell of a corpse down into the museum. Laying him before his mother's niche, I left a stick of incense burning in his folded hands and a pillow of black silk cradling the papery dry bulb of his skull. He would have wished it thus.

The boy has not come to me again, though I leave the window

open every night. I have been back to the club, where I stand sipping vodka and watching the crowd. I have seen many beauties, many strange wasted faces, but not the one I seek. I think I know where I will find him. Perhaps he still desires me—I must know.

I will go again to the lonely graveyard in the bayou. Once more—alone, this time—I will find the unmarked grave and plant my spade in its black earth. When I open the coffin—I know it, I am sure of it!—I will find not the mouldering thing we beheld before, but the calm beauty of replenished youth. The youth he drank from Louis. His face will be a scrimshaw mask of tranquillity. The amulet—I know it; I am sure of it—will be around his neck.

Dying: the final shock of pain or nothingness that is the price we pay for everything. Could it not be the sweetest thrill, the only salvation we can attain...the only true moment of self-knowledge? The dark pools of his eyes will open, still and deep enough to drown in. He will hold out his arms to me, inviting me to lie down with him in his rich wormy bed.

With the first kiss his mouth will taste of wormwood. After that it will taste only of me—of my blood, my life, siphoning out of my body and into his. I will feel the sensations Louis felt: the shriveling of my tissues, the drying-up of all my vital juices. I care not. The treasures and the pleasures of the grave? They are his hands, his lips, his tongue.

Parting Is Such Sweet Sorrow

PAT CALIFIA

Ulrich stood in the living room of his Victorian mansion, using a small crowbar to pry the top and sides off a crate that contained his harpsichord. His long black hair was getting in the way, so he stopped to scrape it back and bind it in a ponytail. If he had been able to sweat, his beard and mustache would have been damp with perspiration. And if water would have done him any good, he would probably be chugging a quart of it by now. Other crates, bearing stickers from Europe, stood nearby, waiting to be unpacked. It was good to be home, back in San Francisco.

Not that Amsterdam had not been fun. The weather was cool and damp and social attitudes were so liberal that sometimes, if he kept his eyes and mind out of focus, he could almost believe that he was still in the city of gaudily painted Victorians and buff young men. It seemed as if the whole gay world had fallen in love with San Francisco and tried to imitate its sensual openness, its lascivious pride. Very little distinguished the adult bookstores with their glory-hole-riddled booths, the backroom bars and the bathhouses in Amsterdam, Paris, Berlin, London and Madrid from the militantly masculine and hopelessly homosexual haunts of Baghdad by the Bay.

But there were always these annoying differences that plucked at Ulrich, distracting him even in the middle of a hunt, and making him homesick for the city where a very butch bartender had helped him to conceal a kill, then warned him not to return until things had cooled off. He would be flirting with a long-haired beauty in a coffee shop, for example, and the man would say something in Dutch. Although cafes in San Francisco reeked of pot smoke too, they didn't have thirteen different brands of hash on a menu posted above the espresso machines. San Francisco had more than its share of erotic entertainment, but nothing like the boy brothels that float-ed down the canals, barges full of choice meat. Ulrich had always been fond of hunting junkies, especially in New York's Alphabet City. He loved their furtiveness and shame. It made any interaction with them seem like espionage. But there was little of that melodrama in Amsterdam, where it was public policy to turn a blind eye to possession of narcotics for personal use. Ulrich never visited the heroin quarter of the city unless he had more on his mind than feeding that day. Nothing bored him more than the posturing of addicts who believed their need set them apart from other people and made them special. Or was it just that he resented the similarity between himself and them, the fact that an analogous hunger drove him with crippling intensity?

The flight over had been stressful. Ulrich's muscles still made cranky comments about being confined inside a trunk. He needed a safe container to protect himself from harm while he slept the sleep of the dead. But during the dark hours of the night, he was as awake as any other man, and it was tedious beyond belief to have nothing to do but count the studs that held the trunk together. The vampire cats who were his guardians and companions had been irate, and refused to entertain him. He might have booked a passenger seat and flown with everyone else, but he was afraid a perky and conscientious stewardess would notice his total lethargy and decide that he was dead. The thought of some self-appointed hero cutting him open with grubby airline cutlery to give him open-heart massage was disgusting.

He had tried flying as a passenger once, but the big dark cloak he had wrapped himself in to sleep had drawn unwanted attention from the other passengers, and they were also startled when he applied duct tape to the window to keep it shut. The controlling powers that normally kept him safe from mortal malice or curiosity didn't function while he was asleep, so he couldn't count on that to make everybody draw their shades and leave him alone. He could endure daylight, but he didn't like it much, and if his sleep was interrupted by the sun, he would awaken in such hunger that no one would deplane alive.

In a similar predicament, Adolpha, his charming (not!) sister, would no doubt have taken one of the many animal forms that were her forte, and simply flown or swam across the ocean under her own steam. Or she would have boarded an ocean liner, stayed on it until she had fed on all the passengers and crew, then sunk the damn thing and taken bird or bat form to wing a few miles to the harbor. With her great power to make people forget what they had seen, Adolpha could afford to be fond of slaughter on a grand scale. But Ulrich had only one animal form, and wolves did not take to the sea like pinnipeds. He could compel people to do things they normally would not do, and make them forget what they had seen, but he shrank from intimate contact with their minds. Perhaps Adolpha was able to alter mortals in a more surgical fashion. Ulrich always found his own mind cluttered by unwelcome bits and pieces of their lives and personalities.

But Adolpha was not here now. Ulrich knew it because he felt happy and comfortable. There had been one vampire in residence, a young and confused prostitute who had probably been created accidentally. At any rate, she had been abandoned by her maker, and it was no problem for Ulrich to dispatch her. He liked killing other vampires, when he didn't know them personally. That sort of blood lasted longer than a day. He might have as much as a week in which he would wake up without feeling the pulsing in his temples and his gut that told him he had to feed right away.

There were other vampires across the bay, in Oakland, in Berkeley. The natural aversion of their kind for one another made vampires space themselves out, as other sorts of predators do, so that each had an adequate territory to meet his or her needs. In cities, where population density was higher, vampires tended to cluster more closely together than they did in smaller towns or rural areas. But Ulrich was famous for forcing other vampires to give him a wide berth. He would tolerate no challenges to his dominance in a city as small and lovely as San Francisco. She belonged to him, her streets were his to caress and her hills were his to embrace. And all her people were under his patronage. The only vampire he could share a city with was his sister, Adolpha, and that was only because when it pleased her to crowd him, there was nothing he could do to stop her.

One nice thing about cities was that people moved around. Ulrich had already checked out his neighbors, and there was only one old man still living there who had seen him during his previous tenancy. It was easy to make him forget someone he had only glimpsed a time or two. So Ulrich kept the same house, rejoicing in the shipments of antique furniture, Persian rugs, and first editions that arrived from Europe. Each time a crate arrived and he opened and unpacked it, he felt as if he were coming home again. Soon everything would look just as it had the night when he had been told to leave San Francisco. Well, plus a harpsichord, a set of originals by Aubrey Beardsley, a Tiffany lamp, and several stained-glass windows that would have to be installed somewhere. You couldn't expect him to be gone for six years and stop shopping. That would be inhumane. He wrestled the musical instrument into a corner and dusted off his hands. The rest of the boxes could be dealt with tomorrow. Night had fallen an hour ago, and he wanted to go out.

The cats were also glad to be back. They loved the back yard of Ulrich's Victorian, and now that it was overgrown, wild creatures had made their home there. They might catch anything, perhaps even a raccoon. "Just leave the skunks alone," he warned them as he let Anastasia, Luna and Hecate out to forage. Russian Blue, Abyssinian and tortoiseshell sent him identical images, cats licking their buttholes with great absorption, to tell him what they thought of his fussing.

Ulrich hoped that no one in his neighborhood let their dog run free. The cats would pack together to hunt an obnoxious canine. Charley was going to be left behind to guard the house while Ulrich went out on reconnaissance. Before he left, the vampire opened a vein in his wrist to let the long-haired black and white tomcat feed. He had blood to spare, thanks to the little streetwalker, and all the cats could use a tonic after being cooped up for so long at high altitudes. He shook his head to rid himself of the memory of her welcoming smile. She had been so glad to see one of her own kind at last, someone who could explain the painful metamorphosis that had changed her body and given her needs she did not understand. She had thought that Ulrich was going to take care of her. The nasty feel of her fake leather jacket, which was actually made out of cheap glossy plastic, still clung to the palms of his hands.

The purring cat at his wrist brought him back to himself. Life was not fair, was it? Even if he had wanted to become her master, Ulrich knew she would have been hopeless as a student. She was not intelligent enough or self-contained enough to endure immortality. And Ulrich was not about to burden himself with responsibility for an inferior. A relationship of that sort was slavery for the ostensibly dominant partner.

He had purchased a new motorcycle yesterday. But before he went to straddle it and conquer the night, Ulrich picked up Charley and held him. He loved the big white ruff that outlined the male cat's chest. His fluffy fur made his big feet look even larger, and between the ebony toes sprouted tufts of more white fur. The cat had a long spray of thick white whiskers that pricked Ulrich's face. Charley went limp in his arms, a sure sign of deep contentment. Ulrich sometimes carried him around the house for hours, over his shoulder, while Charley purred and drooled. Ulrich hoarded the feeling of Charley's vibrating body against his chest, storing up the animal's deep love for him in his own undying heart. In a mental picture that included smells as well as visuals, Charley told Ulrich that he loved him as much as a bowl full of goldfish, though he would love him even more once the fish tank was set up. The amorality and pitiless nature of the cats were a great comfort to Ulrich. They took the sort of joy in life eternal that sometimes eluded their formerly human caretaker.

Ulrich put Charley down and dusted cat hair off his leathers. The last time he had been here, he had gone in for a lot of fringe, if memory served. Now he was into a sleeker look, and wore an expensive, body-hugging racer's jumpsuit. It was amazing how persistent cat fur was. How often had he interrupted a killing bite so he could brush a cat hair from his victim's neck? Almost reluctantly, he went to the garage to start his brand-new bike. It was strange to travel out into the world without being driven by the great hunger. He almost wanted to stay home and putter with his things, alphabetize his tapes and albums, reshelve the books according to topic, author and age. But he knew what he had really come to San Francisco to do. He had come to see Alain, the bartender whose shotgun blast had obliterated the signs of Ulrich's feeding on the body of a young man who had been snatched from the urinals and taken into the alley to provide his nightly feast. He still got goosebumps when he remembered the cool tones of Alain's voice, informing him that the kills he had scored in the Eagle's Lair had been good for business. It wasn't like a mortal to see him in a positive light, or have such callous feelings toward his own kind.

Over the centuries, Ulrich had frequently sought companionship and understanding from mortals. All he needed to palliate the isolation, he told himself, was one companion, one other person who saw him as he really was, and accepted him in all his ambiguity. Not one of these experiments had been a success. Christianity had poisoned the entire Western world. Even mortals who thought they were atheists or freethinkers reverted to the superstitious catechism of their childhood and saw Ulrich as a demon, an emissary of Satan Himself. Not that prayers or crucifixes could stop a pagan like Ulrich. As the West became more secular, people did not stop seeing the vampire as an evil supernatural entity. They just stopped seeing him at all. Most of them did not believe in vampires until they actually felt his sharp teeth penetrate their flesh. Then they struggled, until his strong hands crushed their flesh. Ulrich thought it was an odd way to find religion, but then, Christianity had always paid more attention to evil than to good. Christian vampires, now there were some awful people. Guilt-ridden, afraid of garlic and mirrors and crosses, burned by holy water (as if all water was not holy), they usually rushed headlong toward their own destruction like a runaway train. And they had awful taste in clothes. Belief was such a powerful thing. Ulrich often wondered what assumptions he made that limited his own life.

Unlike a hundred other mortals who panicked or denied his true nature, Alain had seen him. And he had not flinched, not turned away, not denied the truth or tried to run from it. Surely six years was enough time to let the titillating scandal about a South of Market murderer subside. Alain had said he could come back. And Ulrich wanted to see him, but he was also afraid. Mortals changed so much in such a short time. Besides, Ulrich knew nothing about him except that he was a bartender at the Eagle's Lair. He didn't even know his last name.

Lacking any other place to start, he went back to his old haunts South of Market. The new Harley handled easily, and Ulrich realized the BMW he had been driving in Amsterdam had needed its front fork aligned. Oh, well. The student he had tossed the keys and papers to would have to worry about that. Ulrich was at the Eagle's Lair before he was aware of much time passing. Unfortunately, the place was now boarded up, the sign faded, the backroom no doubt full of ghosts who still hadn't found a trick for the night. Shit. This quest wasn't going to be as smoothly plotted as a Falcon video, was it?

Ulrich turned the bike and went down Folsom Street, looking for other places he remembered. Most of them had closed their doors. A few of the bars had simply changed their names. The Combat Zone was The OK Corral now, and Ulrich shuddered as he listened to the country music that poured out of its doors as faux cowboys came and went. Appalling stuff, that, the aural equivalent of possum cooked in molasses. The boots were nice, though. Colorful. Ulrich had always liked a bit more of a heel on his boots than this century found appropriate for men.

Finally he spotted another man on the street who was wearing leather. Two men, actually, a well-groomed couple in their forties. The top was in leather pants, a leather uniform shirt, and a cap with a thin chain about its brim. The bottom was in chaps and a leather vest, and had a thicker chain draped loosely around his neck. Under the chaps he wore a jock strap, nothing else. Ulrich made a little face. What use was a collar that did not lock? Still, these men were the closest he had seen to brothers in an hour and a half of searching, so he let his bike drift to a crawl beside them and said, "Good evening."

"Evening," the top said, turning to face him. Ulrich adored his gray handlebar mustache and big sideburns. The pocket of the uniform shirt bulged with hefty brown cigars, which smelled wonderful but did not compensate for the lack of a big bulge further down. The bottom turned also and waited a little behind his master, although he leaned over to make sure he got a good look at Ulrich's body. *Smack that boy,* Ulrich thought impatiently, then focused his attention once more on the older of the two.

"I just got into town," he explained. "Where's the party? Seems like it's been hidden pretty good."

The top chuckled. "Eager for action, huh?"

Ulrich gave him a look that would have made him step back if he was any smarter. "Oh, yes," he said finally. "Action."

"Well, you can't do any better than the Bear Cave," the man with the bodacious mustache said. "But it's not on the main drag." He gave Ulrich directions to a side street. "We're headed that way ourselves," he said, and put a hand out to drag his boy forward. "Wait for us, and we'll buy you a drink. Welcome you to San Francisco in style."

Ulrich did not say yes or no. He just nodded, raised his hand, and sped away. Could it be that in this thriving queer metropolis there was only one leather bar? What had happened to this town? Back in 1975, he had been aware that many of the butch men who stood around in hundreds of dollars worth of cowhide couldn't wait to take all that hot, cumbersome clothing off the minute they got home with a trick. The number of sadomasochists, as opposed to the number of men who simply liked the masculine look of leather, had been small. Could it be that leather was no longer a fashionable fad? Was he going to have to go hunting in preppy sweater bars?

Shuddering at that humiliating thought, Ulrich raced to the location the couple on Folsom Street had given him. He parked his bike between a little Suzuki and a good-sized Yamaha that had seen better days and went in, eager to inhale the scent of beer, cigar smoke, piss and sweat that colored and thickened the air of such places.

There it was in abundance, and Ulrich's nostrils drank it in like wine. He took off his gloves, tucked them under the epaulet of his jacket, and went to the bar. There were two men behind it, but neither of them were Alain. He ordered a single-malt scotch that he could not drink, just to enjoy the incense of its fiery aroma. The young man who brought it was pretty in a common way, and clearly thought himself a great beauty. The silver bar pinned to his leather vest read *Billy*. Ulrich scanned the patrons of the bar, and was bitterly disappointed to see that Alain was not among them. He got the bartender's attention again by holding out a fifty-dollar bill, and leaned toward his ear. "I'm looking for somebody," he said, and the upstart laughed.

"You came to the right place," the bartender said, and made a grand gesture that included everyone in the place.

"No," Ulrich said emphatically, slamming one hand on the bar. Billy jumped away. Ulrich summoned him closer with a crooked finger. "I am looking for a particular man," Ulrich hissed. "An old friend. Someone I lost touch with a few years ago. I need to find him now." He gave Billy the limited information he had, and was delighted to see comprehension dawn in those weakly handsome features.

"Why, that's one of the owners," Billy said. "He doesn't come around much any more. Sometimes he's here on weekends."

"Where does he live?" Ulrich demanded.

"Well, I can't just give you his address," Billy protested. "I mean, I'm not even sure I know it. It would be worth my job to give you his telephone number."

"Then give him mine," Ulrich said through clenched teeth, and wrote it down on one of the cards the bar provided its customers. It said, *Here I am falling in love with you and I don't even know your name* _____ *or telephone number* _____. Billy took the card with the tips of his fingers, and Ulrich suddenly knew that he was in love with Alain and not about to pass another man's telephone number on to him. As if this puppy could endure what Alain's lust demanded! Furious, Ulrich went into the young man's mind, and took the information he wanted.

But first, he found out that the bartender had about six more months to live. His death would have something to do with the red marks upon his chest, marks that looked almost like bruises, except that they were raised. Coming back to himself, Ulrich had an ugly moment in which the vapid face behind the bar had turned into a grinning skull. He turned away to escape this macabre vision, and the consciousness he had opened was invaded by information about everyone in the bar.

All of these men were sick. Well, not all of them. Perhaps half a dozen were whole. But the rest would die sometime over the next year, mostly of pneumonia. Ulrich turned and almost ran for the door. He collided with the couple who had directed him to the Bear Cave, and knew for a fact that the master would barely have time to bury his boy before he himself was in the hospital, dying of an infection that was not supposed to be fatal, something he caught from the tropical birds he loved to keep.

It normally took a lot to turn Ulrich's stomach, but this onslaught of death in a place where he had hoped to renew his own life was just too much. He muttered an incoherent apology to the master, handed his boy back to him, and darted out the door.

"Daddy, what's wrong with that man?" the boy asked.

"I don't know, son," said the master. "I'd rather know he's crazy now, though, than find out after we took him home. Go get your old man a beer, now, and try to do it without shaking your ass at every big dick in this place."

It took Ulrich two tries to start his Harley. Too bad the people who made these things could never get certain details right, like making them start up when you turned the key. Finally he kicked it alive, and the violent gesture calmed him down. Some of the shaking went away as the big bike's vibrations went through his hands, up his arms, and into the rest of his body. He went back to Folsom, got his bearings, and took Howard Street back toward the Eagle's Lair. Alain had bought a building close to the bar. There were three apartments in the building. He lived on the top floor.

Ulrich parked outside the somewhat dilapidated facade of the building and went to the front door. There were buzzers for each apartment, but the front door was unlocked, so he simply went in. The stairs were a nuisance, but he bolted up them, more and more angry with himself for staying away so long. Why let Alain send him away in the first place, hmm? Vampire reflexes were so much quicker than mortal ones, it wouldn't have been that risky to take the gun away from him. If only he had dragged Alain out of the alley and taken him home! When you lived forever, it was too easy to lose touch with mortal frailty, the brevity of their lifespans. Ulrich cursed himself in the medieval German dialect of his boyhood, a language he used only when he was very upset or surprised.

Then he was at Alain's front door, and he did not know what to do. He wanted to break it down, but that would be crass, and might attract unwanted attention. He gently rattled the knob. This door was locked. Ulrich shrugged and rapped it hard with his knuckles.

There was no response. But he could feel warmth inside the apartment, the heat of a human body. So he knocked again, more sharply this time, leaning into it. Someone on the other side opened the door abruptly, and Ulrich stumbled in.

"What's your goddamned hurry?" Alain snapped, then he saw who had troubled his day off. "Well, speak of the devil," he said in an awed tone of voice, and grinned. Ulrich found himself being picked up and vigorously hugged, an embrace that would have cracked a normal man's ribs. Then Alain was kissing him, the black stubble on his cheeks scraping Ulrich's face. His tongue was big, his mouth tasted like sex and cigar smoke. Ulrich petted his shaved head (more coarse black stubble there) and massaged the big muscles in Alain's broad shoulders. He had not been wearing a shirt, just a pair of dirty 501's, so Ulrich could run his hands down the planes of muscle that outlined his back. There were more tattoos than there had been when they last met, and the rings in Alain's nipples were a bigger gauge.

When Alain was done smooching him, he put him down, and Ulrich gasped. He had not been able to expand his chest to draw a full breath for several minutes. Alain was talking a mile a minute, and Ulrich was having trouble following it all. The phrase "you bastard" appeared frequently. "How the hell did you ever find me?" Alain demanded.

"The Bear Cave—Billy—" he gasped, and Alain nodded.

"I should can his weasly little ass for handing out personal information, but I'm so goddamned glad to see you, it can wait until tomorrow. What can I get you? I know it's early, but let's have a drink. Or would you rather smoke a little bud?"

Ulrich gave him a look that said "be real."

"Oh, no, I guess you wouldn't." Alain stood three feet away, chewing his full lower lip, trying to think of some other form of hospitality he could offer his strange visitor. Ulrich had a few moments to examine the furnishings of the room, which were simple but expensive, all the furniture made of oak and upholstered in brown leather. While he was distracted, Alain advanced upon him, embraced him a little more gently this time, and began to unzip his leathers. "Get your clothes off, man," he said impatiently. "I'm not going to let you get away this time."

If Ulrich had been able to weep, he would have been in tears. His sexual encounters with mortals had been brief, controlled affairs. It was hard to let go when you had to keep your true nature a secret. Thank the horned god for the vampire blood he had ingested less than two days ago. It made it possible for him to be erect between Alain's hands without feeding on him first. The experience of being undressed and fondled was terrifying. Ulrich found himself hyperventilating, straining to get away and straining to get closer to the big man who had gone straight to the heart of a hunger that was much more difficult to satisfy than a mere need for blood.

Then Alain had picked him up again and was taking him into another room. Ulrich once again felt the panicky sensation of wanting to escape and wanting to have this moment last forever. He was being held, comforted, practically abducted by a handsome, brutal man who knew he was a vampire and wanted him anyway. He stared wildly around the room, trying to distract himself. It was a cross between a bedroom and a dungeon. There was equipment hanging on all of the walls, workmanlike stuff that was obviously used frequently. There were a couple of posters, framed, from bars that Ulrich remembered, places where he had found sweet young men who tasted of springtime and workouts in the gym. On his way into the room, Alain had punched a button on his tape player, and the big reel had started to turn, surrounding them with the spacy sound effects and insistent beat of queer disco, the kind of raunchy, high-tech music straight people were afraid to dance to.

Alain dumped him on the bed, wound his hands in Ulrich's long, black hair, and stretched out on top of him. By the way their bodies sank into the mattress, Ulrich guessed it was a waterbed. Heated, fortunately. Then Alain was kissing him again, taking the time to do it right, and Ulrich almost came from the wonderful feeling of having his mouth explored with so much ruthless tenderness. He dared to put his hand on the buttons of Alain's fly and ease them out of their holes. When he palmed Alain's erection, the bartender groaned and dug his tongue so deeply into Ulrich's mouth, he was about to hit his tonsils. Ulrich had seen Alain's cock a time or two, years before, when he took a piss at the Eagle's Lair. The Prince Albert was still there, the thick ring that went through his piss-hole and came out just below the rim of his cock head. But he also had a series of smaller rings that went down the underside of his cock, and a couple in his ballsac. Figuring anybody who liked to get pierced this much wouldn't be able to do without a certain classic ornament, Ulrich reached a little further back and found the guiche that pierced Alain's perineum. When he tugged on it, Alain's cock jumped, and his precum stained Ulrich's thighs.

His own cock was painfully rigid. Alain was stroking it with one hand, and ran his thumb across the head. Ulrich made himself meet Alain's gaze, saw the question that made one of his eyebrows go up. "I don't do that," he explained. "I mean, I come, and I come really hard, but it's dry. No jizz."

Alain shrugged and began to play with Ulrich's nipples. His broad thumbs were capable of small, delicate motions, and Ulrich felt his pelvis lurching forward, toward Alain, driven by the arousal that was heating up his chest. Alain, sadist that he was, quit toying with Ulrich's nipples and stuck his fingers in his mouth. He felt his pointed fangs, then stuck another finger in, and moved them in and out. "Did you ever think of getting your tongue pierced?" Alain asked. "It's already a wild trip, kissing you with those big, sharp canines. But a ball in your tongue would be too much, I'd come just from swapping spit with you."

"I don't know if my body would hold a piercing," Ulrich said, trying to sound thoughtful and objective. The truth was that the idea of it frightened him to death (well, not quite that much). "Does it hurt much?" he asked, trying not to sound as timid as he was.

Alain wasn't fooled, and laughed so hard, Ulrich thought he might suffer internal damage. "Oh, what a big old chicken you are," Alain guffawed. "Mister Nightmare, creeping around in shadows, has to catch and kill his own dinner every goddamned day, and he's afraid to get a little old needle stuck through his tongue. What would you do if I made a big fucking hole in the head of your dick, Ulrich? Pass out on me?"

Ulrich hid his head against Alain's chest and swore he was blushing. "I hate you," he said.

"Well, of course you do," Alain said comfortably. "Everybody I bring into this room comes to hate me sooner or later. Why else do you think I do it? Nothing makes my cock get harder than that cold stare of pure hostility, when I know if a guy could get loose he'd break my neck. Except he can't get away, all he can do is rage against me, and he's so frustrated he's ready to cry. Pure gold, that is pure gold. Better than a case of champagne or a pile of cocaine. So, scaredy-cat, get your nose down there and lick around those big old rings of mine. If you can't stand the thought of getting a few of your own, you better admire the ones that I've got."

Ulrich was happy to oblige. He slid the head of Alain's cock into his mouth and down his throat, carefully guiding the shaft so that it ran between his fangs. It wasn't easy to keep from puncturing or scratching it. None of Ulrich's teeth were dull. But he wrapped his lips around them, trying to cushion their edges. He didn't care if he cut his own mouth up a little in the process. His tongue was equally problematic; it was thin and raspy, more of a file than a human tongue. But Alain seemed to enjoy the way it felt, moving back and forth on the underside of his dick. If he thought about it, Ulrich would have had to admit that he was not protecting Alain from the sensation of having his cock scored. Anybody with this much gold in his equipment would probably love to be nibbled by vampire teeth. He was protecting himself from Alain's blood, and from the unwelcome knowledge it might contain.

Alain rapped him on top of his head. "Quit daydreamin' and tend to business," he snapped.

Ulrich obeyed. Soon he was rewarded by a dose of hot cum that nearly choked him. Alain hauled him up so they were face-to-face and licked off the spit and white stuff that had spattered Ulrich's mustache and beard. "I always like to come before I play," Alain murmured in his ear. "It makes me so much meaner if I'm not distracted by a hard dick. Know what I mean?"

Ulrich did not know, but he was certainly trying to figure it out now. Alain interrupted this anxious reverie. "So, tell me about yourself," he said, tugging on Ulrich's hair to force his head back and focus his eyes on Alain's face.

"What do you want to know?" Ulrich replied.

"Don't be a smartass." Alain tightened his grip on Ulrich's hair and slapped him lightly on one cheek.

"I'm honestly not being flippant," Ulrich said patiently, relishing the smart along one side of his face. "I don't know what you are planning. I don't know what you need to know. Ask me questions, and I will answer them honestly."

"Stand up," Alain said, and roughly dragged him off the bed and onto his feet. Ulrich played along, allowing himself to be manhandled. It was delicious to be able to pretend he was out of control. Alain handed him a piece of chain. "Can you break that?" he demanded.

"Of course not," Ulrich said, relishing the way each cool link slid through his hands, like the scales on snakeskin. But he could not look Alain in the eye and say it, and the master sensed his lie. For that, he was kicked to the floor.

"Don't jerk me around, grab that chain and show me just how strong you are," Alain said impatiently.

Ulrich shrugged, yanked the chain taut, and snapped it like a piece of string. "I'm sorry," he said, when he saw Alain's look of disbelief.

"Bend over the horse," Alain said, not acknowledging his apology.

Ulrich went on his knees to the piece of equipment Alain indicated, stood, and bent over it. The padded surface was comfortable and sturdy enough to make him feel quite secure. "I'm going to hit you with something," Alain said. "You tell me how it feels." A braided cat-o'-nine-tails landed hard across his shoulders. Ulrich sighed happily. "Well?" Alain said impatiently, poised for another blow.

"It's hard to know what to say," Ulrich said sadly. "It's been a long time since I was changed, and there are so many things I've forgotten. And other things I don't know how to describe, since you have never experienced them. I'm not very sensitive to pain. I don't need to be, my body can repair almost any injury. That insensitivity helps me to ignore the risk to myself when I go out to feed. When you hit me, I know it should hurt, but it doesn't exactly. It's more as if it makes me remember what it is to hurt."

"Well, goddammit, that sucks," Alain said. Ulrich knew without looking that he would be chewing his lower lip.

"I want you," Ulrich said. "I've wanted you for years. Think of it this way, Alain. You can do your worst with me."

"You've got my attention now," Alain said. "Go on."

"Haven't you ever wanted to go as far as you could? You're a sadist, Alain. But you're smart about it. You don't go around kidnapping and torturing strangers. You ask for permission. You prefer men who don't have a lot of limits, but you stay within those boundaries. But surely you've wondered about it. What are *your* limits, Alain? I'm willing to bet that no bottom has ever been able to give you carte blanche. And I'm hungry for this. Think about how horny you get if you've got to do without sex for two weeks. Then imagine what it would be like to be me. I'm a creature of physical, sensual appetites, Alain. That's all that I am. I live to satisfy the cravings of my body. I manage to get a few other things done from time to time, but mostly I exist to feed, to feel the pleasure that comes from satisfying that hunger. But I have other appetites, just like you do, and this has never happened to me before. I've never had this opportunity. It's been centuries, Alain. If you tell me to stand inside your chains and leave them unbroken, I will do that. I will. You are the only person here who needs to set any limits. Not me."

Alain gave him a sharp look. "That sounds too good to be true. So there's nothing that can permanently damage you or threaten your life? You're just immortal, you live forever, nothing can kill you?"

Ulrich had thought he was completely open to this man, and would hold nothing back from him. But he balked at answering this question.

"I thought so. Well, that's okay. We've all got our little secrets. I like secrets. Just promise me you won't hate yourself when I make you give it up. I'm going to take you up on your offer, Ulrich. I haven't been this horny for months. Don't know what's been wrong with me, ever since this winter I haven't been myself." Alain shook himself like a wet dog. "Well, nothing's more boring than having to listen to somebody whine about their health like a senile old lady." He took Ulrich by the shoulders and guided him to a wall where chains dangled from heavy eyebolts that were sunk deep into the building's supporting timbers. He wrapped the chains around Ulrich's wrists and secured them with large padlocks. "No need to protect your nerves and tendons with a pair of wrist cuffs, is there?" he jeered. "So, just to make this official, I'm telling you: Leave those chains alone. If one of them breaks, I'll find a way to make you sorry. It's a tough order to find a way to punish somebody like you, but I've got a few tricks up my sleeve that might surprise you."

Ulrich bowed his head and waited while Alain sorted through the whips that hung from a circular cast-iron frame that was probably manufactured for gourmet chefs to hang up their anodized aluminum pans. His sharp hearing caught Alain murmuring under his breath. "Forget that, too light. Too candy-assed. Ha, ha, don't need to bother with that bugger. Well, fuck all. I don't need to warm him up at all, do I? Goddamn. Let's see. What have I got that's really effective? Yes, you, and you, and you. You too. Come to the party, babies, Daddy's about to have himself a *good* time."

Alain began with a wire brush that he'd bought at an auto supply store. Ulrich supposed it was used to clean machine parts. The brass bristles were sharp and stiff. Alain pulverized the skin over his shoulders, back, butt and thighs. It felt to Ulrich like lying out naked under a hail storm. There was more of a feeling of pressure than anything else, although occasionally a bright thin spatter of pain would penetrate his consciousness.

"Yesss," Alain hissed. "Gonna have myself a *good* time."

A rubber cat was next. The heavy latex cords had been tipped with metal nuts, knotted to hold them in place. This made Ulrich grunt a bit. It was a nice, deep massage. Then he felt Alain's hands all over his back and butt, smearing thick liquid across his skin. "Baby," Alain said gently, "you're a mess. Let me make it all better," and turned his head to kiss him. The kiss created far more sensation than the beating. Ulrich drank it in, giddy with pleasure. Alain was full of fierce joy, and it made Ulrich happy to be able to put him in that altered state.

Other implements followed. It made Alain cheerful to show him each one before using it, and tell him a little story about where it had come from and how it had been used in the past (if ever). The truck antenna had been set into a steel handle by a tool-and-die worker in Seattle who promised Alain he would make him a new one if it ever broke. Alain had managed to bend it on its maker, but it remained intact. The little flail tipped with hooks was something Alain made himself to frighten away a persistent would-be slave who was not his type. The beautifully shaped wooden club was acquired on a fishing trip. (It was made to knock out big salmon.) Until now, it had mostly been used to fuck boys who wanted something bigger than a dick up their asses.

Ulrich's feet slipped. He was apparently standing in a puddle of his own fluids. Alain was growing progressively more and more excited. Finally he left Ulrich's side and came back with a black-snake, six feet long. "If this won't make you dance for me, nothing will," Alain declared, and let it snap.

This was not a massage. This was a slicing caress, with just enough of an edge to it to make Ulrich wonder if it was pleasure or pain. The novel sensation made him crazy. He panted, whined for it, and almost forgot his vow to leave the chains unbroken, just because he was so excited. Again and again Alain let him taste the snakebite edge of the long braided whip, until Ulrich was biting his own lips and crying, "More, more, more!"

But before he had enough, Alain was at his side, unlocking the padlocks and catching his limp body, turning him around, locking him up again so he faced out from the wall. He drew a Bowie knife from a scabbard that ran down his right thigh. It was a monster knife, Ulrich thought. Not quite big enough to be a bayonet or a sword, but definitely longer than the four-inch limit on a legal pocketknife. "Remember," Alain said evenly, "I told you not to break those chains. And you told me you would obey me. Do you have honor? The point of the knife came to rest between Ulrich's nipples, slightly to the left of his breastbone. Ulrich whined at the sight of it, but Alain was still talking. "And if you have honor, how far does it go?" he asked thoughtfully. The point of the knife went into Ulrich's body a full half-inch. "Far enough to trust me with your precious overextended life?" Alain wondered.

Ulrich was shrieking, rattling the chains that he had given his word to leave intact. Alain's face was set in a snarl, the lips drawn back in exactly the same fashion that Ulrich's cleared his teeth when he was ready to drink. To the excited vampire's senses, Alain's hand seemed to draw back in slow motion. This was it, the killing stroke, the knife to the heart that could end his life. Ulrich found himself howling in his wolf-voice, driven by desperation back to the animal part of his nature, and then the knife arced forward—

And lodged in his chest only a quarter of an inch away from his heart. Alain pulled it out, and a spout of blood hit him in the chest. The two men stood facing one another, panting, marked by a nearly identical gout of blood. Then Alain sheathed his knife, laughed a little at both of them, and released the padlocks. Ulrich allowed himself to fall into his arms. By the spear of the Sky Father, he had never been so scared.

Alain half-carried, half-threw Ulrich face down onto the bed and shoved a big piece of Crisco up his ass. Ulrich's ability to feel pleasure was the opposite of his numbness to pain. His predator's body was more sensitive to arousal than mortal flesh. It seemed as if he could feel every vein on Alain's swollen cock, and he could certainly feel the outline of every single ring that pierced his dick. By the time Alain had gone in and out of him a half-dozen times, Ulrich swore he could have told you the gauge of each piece of jewelry. Never had he been fucked like this, with so much dedication and determination. Alain reached around in front of him, hauled him to his knees, and wrapped his fingers around Ulrich's cock. With the big tool lodged firmly in his guts, Ulrich shouted from the intensity of the pleasure he felt as Alain jacked him off again and again.

"Tell me you want it," Alain said, slightly out of breath, the words jerky because of the pounding he was giving Ulrich's ass. "Tell me you want my cum, cocksucker. Tell me how bad you want it. Beg for it or I'll pull out, I swear I will."

Ulrich was surprised by the little speech he made. Who would have guessed he could be that abject, or that poetic? Apparently it was effective, because Alain came hard, and Ulrich's thirsty flesh drank up each drop of the white blood.

And now he knew. He had known since Alain came in his mouth, but he had been too impatient, distracted by his own hard cock, to let the information sink in. Alain had it, whatever it was. He was doomed.

They snuggled together on the bed, Ulrich sticking to the leather bedspread. "We made quite a mess," he said fondly.

"I feel wonderful," Alain exclaimed. "I haven't been so happy since Kip died. He was a hell of a masochist, but nothing like you, baby. My arms are burning like I bench-pressed three hundred pounds."

"Kip was your boy?" Ulrich asked.

"No, he hated all that role-playing shit. He just liked to turn up at my house once a week, down half a bottle of Jack Daniels, and get the shit kicked out of him. No games. He was a good man and a good friend."

Ulrich didn't want to ask, but found himself voicing a question anyway. "How did he go?"

"Some weird-assed kind of pneumonia that the doctors couldn't cure. Or at least that's what they said. I think they just didn't give a damn. He was just some fag to them. What did they care if he died?"

"So he had it too," Ulrich said, then wanted to cut his own throat.

"Huh?" Alain knew he had heard something important, and he would not let Ulrich take it back. Eventually he got the whole story out of him: Billy, the skull face, the premature mortality looming over the patrons of the bar. Then, of course, he wanted to know, "What about me?"

Ulrich could not answer him directly. "I could make you like me," he said.

Alain studied him coldly. "So you can tell I'm sick, even though I feel fine?"

Ulrich nodded.

Alain thought it over. "So what would that mean? You have to feed every day, right?"

"Usually," Ulrich said. "Unless I've fed on another vampire. Then I can go for a few days without mortal blood."

"So you guys don't hang together? There's no fraternal bond?"

"No, there's not." Ulrich's body was still singing from the pleasure this man had given to him, and he could not withhold the information he needed to make a decision. "We can't tolerate each other, in fact. Vampires don't like to be around other hunters. We need to keep a certain zone of space between us."

"So you and I would not be spending eternity playing perverted leather games with one another?"

Ulrich shook his head.

"And you say it's bad? Everybody's got it?"

Ulrich nodded. "These things happen periodically, Alain. I've seen lots of plagues sweep through the human population and decimate it, about once every hundred years or so. This one is too new to have a name yet, but it's every bit as nasty as bubonic plague or the Black Death or cholera. Millions of people will die."

"Including all of my friends. My God. In a few more years, San Francisco will be a ghost town. Do you have any idea what we've built here, Ulrich? How many men have sacrificed careers and their families and come here to make this a gay Mecca? This is the only place on earth where we can be ourselves and live without fear. We have this city by the balls." He took his arm out from under Ulrich's body but stayed close to him, stroking his chest. Ulrich waited patiently for him to speak again.

"I killed somebody once," Alain said finally. The confession came out in awkward bits and pieces. "A basher. I was cruising this rest area down on the interstate, and I blew this big trucker. Got up in his cab to do him, just like some kind of Jack Fritscher fantasy. Motherfucker came at me with a tire iron when I was done. If he hadn't gotten himself a really great blowjob before he tried to kill me, I probably wouldn't have been so pissed off. I might have just run away. But the nerve of him, to get his dick sucked and then turn all self-righteous and call *me* a queer? Forget that shit. I took that tire iron away from him and beat his head in. Took it home, washed it off, kept it in the trunk of my car. I've still got it. That's weird, huh?"

"How did you feel about it?" Ulrich wanted to know.

"Well, that's an interesting question. I guess I had fantasized about it often enough, what it would be like to kill someone. Because, of course, you know that's what I'm supposed to be all about. If I like to hurt people I must secretly be a killer. But it made me sick. I threw up for about an hour. And then I went to sleep for two days. I don't think I liked it much. Certainly didn't give me a boner. I was just glad to be alive myself. And pissed at him for getting me in a corner."

"It's different when you feel the hunger," Ulrich said, yawning. How far away was dawn?

Alain put out his hand and grabbed one of the big canines. Ulrich let him, loving the feeling of having this man put his hands in his mouth. "I'll just bet it is," he whispered. "But I don't think I want to find out." Ulrich stared at him, stricken. "I know you mean it kindly," Alain said gently, withdrawing his hand. "But my whole life is about fucking other men. I gave up everything in order to have a life where I do whatever gets me hard. My family is the men who come to me to get tied up and spit on and beaten and fucked. I don't want to live long enough to see the end of what we've made here. I can't stand the thought of watching them die and leave me behind. It makes me too sad. And I couldn't do what you've done, Ulrich. I couldn't wait a year to get my rocks off, much less a century."

"Feeding is very pleasurable," Ulrich argued. "I wish I could show you how it feels, Alain. It's—"

"It's lonely," Alain said flatly, and Ulrich knew the verdict was final. For the first time in his immortal life, he felt what might have been tears in the corners of his eyes. Alain reached out and wiped them away, and Ulrich saw the bloody traces on his fingers. "I could make you," he said fiercely. "I could force you to drink my blood. And I should do it, I should, I should!"

Alain pinned the clenched fists that were beating on his chest. "No, you shouldn't, baby." Alain gathered him up and patted him on the back, treating him like a mourning child. "I know you love me, and you want to keep me with you, Ulrich, but that's just not in the cards." He kissed him on the nose, and the fond gesture made Ulrich weep again, painful thin strands of diluted blood.

"There's one thing you can do for me. Two, actually," Alain said.

"What—is it?" Ulrich hiccuped.

Alain got a firm grip on his bearded chin. "Let me put a big fuckin' stud in your tongue, honey. Then I want you to fuck me. It's been a long time since I met a man whose dick I wanted up my ass. Then bite me, and let me go when I'm in your arms, doing the stuff I love the best."

"Are you sure?" Ulrich demanded.

"Yes, I'm sure. Now let me get up and deal with a couple of things. No, you stay in bed." Ulrich watched from the leather-covered waterbed, which was gently rocking from the sudden absence of Alain's bulk. He was moving decisively through his apartment, pulling a few things together: a manila envelope ("my last will and testament"), some keys ("this here's the truck, this here is to the bar, and that's the summer cabin on the Russian River"), a locked strongbox ("somebody oughta get rid of all this primo dope before the cops arrive"), and some jewelry ("won't ever have to pawn my diamonds to get out of the country now"). He sat on the edge of the bed and wrote a note on the manila envelope. *Harvey*, it said, *you probably won't believe this, but it was the best time I ever had. Everything in here belongs to you. I love you, man, take care. Throw me a hell of a going-away party. P.S. Fire Billy.* Alain signed his name, then went away, presumably to leave everything on the kitchen table.

He stuck his head in the door and gestured for Ulrich to come out. "The light's better out here," he said. The kitchen was well-lit, furnished with a yellow Formica table and some buttercup yellow chairs that matched. "Pretty queeny, huh?" Alain said, and got him to sit down in one of the chairs. There was a surgical drape on the table, a needle, and a few different studs. "Stick out your tongue," Alain said, and grabbed it with a pair of forceps. The stick wasn't too bad. Ulrich crossed his eyes so he couldn't see it coming. But it made his eyes tingle. The thick post in his tongue was a trip, the stud pressing against the roof of his mouth. He supposed he would get used to it in time.

"Now you belong to me," Alain said, clapping him on the shoulder. "You don't know how many times I've had men beg me to wear my rings and be my property, Ulrich. You are the only one who's gotten me to do it. Now a little bit of me will be with you every time you punch open some poor fucker's neck and drink him dry. Feed for my sake, buddy."

Alain just stood there looking at him, and Ulrich felt unaccountably shy. "Thanks," he muttered, looking at the toes of his bare feet. Then he looked up at Alain again, and marveled at the man's sheer ballsiness. Anybody else who had heard Ulrich's bad news would have shrugged it off. They would have preferred denial to a cold confrontation with the certainty of their own death. But Alain faced it the same way he had faced the revelation of Ulrich, standing over a bled-white body, fangs out, hunger not quite sated. He saw things as they were, and if they were weird, that simply excited him. His first question about any novel fact seemed to be, What unique sexual opportunities lie in this bizarre event?

Ulrich decided that he did not care if dawn was pending. He put away his own sorrow and sealed it in a deep, dark, faraway place. He could mourn later, when it would not taint Alain's last hours. It was the face he had seen bending over the boy's body in the alley that Alain wanted to see now. From somewhere, Ulrich found the strength to become his most amoral, ferocious self. He was up off the chair and had Alain by the throat before the big man even saw him coming. "So you like to pick people up," Ulrich sneered, and lifted him with one hand. "You like to make other men think they are helpless." He shook Alain like a woman shakes out a tablecloth. "Let me show you what it's like to be helpless. Let me show you, oh, all kinds of interesting things."

They were back in the bedroom, and Ulrich bound him face down to the bed the way he had been bound to the wall, with chains wrapped around wrists and ankles and padlocked in place. The coroner wouldn't have to think much to figure out where those marks came from. He went to the cast-iron carousel full of whips and picked out a handful. Alain had good taste. There was no junk in his collection. Everything was well-made, the braids tight, the leather well-cared for. Ulrich had hidden out during the French Revolution in a brothel where he dressed as an aristocrat and flogged Citizen Fraternité, Égalité and Liberté, who felt a little guilty about chopping off the king's head. It was pleasant to have such carefully crafted whips in his hands again.

"I don't believe I asked for all this," Alain said menacingly from his spread-eagled position on the bed.

"Like I care," Ulrich retorted, and lashed out. "You have wanted this from me since you first laid eyes on me. And you are not leaving this world until you have taken everything that I feel like handing out."

The beating he administered was thorough, but tempered with mercy. Alain did not have the experience or the tolerance of a devoted bottom. Still, he took more than Ulrich would have gambled on. One of the things he loved about gay men in this city, and in this era, was their shamelessness. Top or bottom, when they saw or felt something they liked, they went for it wholeheartedly, without apology. Alain liked what he was feeling. Ulrich worked him up to a frenzy, then tossed the whips aside, unchained him, and turned him onto his back.

"Are you ready?" Ulrich asked, but Alain was already greasing up his cock, which responded as if it had not been milked dozens of times already this evening. Ulrich settled on his knees between Alain's spread thighs, and rested the other man's feet on his own shoulders. "Just hang on me," he said. "Don't worry about holding yourself up. I'll hold you up."

Then he picked up Alain's torso, and slid him onto his cock. It was hot in there and tight, which pleased Ulrich a great deal.

Apparently Alain had not been lying about the fact that this was a rare experience. "Does it feel good, baby?" he asked the other man, who had spread his arms out like Jesus on the cross.

"Yeah, oh, yeah," Alain moaned, eyes rolled back in his head.

"Think about this," Ulrich warned. "Think about what you're giving up. This beautiful body that feels so good when I touch it here and pinch it here. The feel of my fat dick taking you on a good hard ride. My lips." He kissed the other man, broke off the kiss, fucked him a little harder, a little faster. "Can you say good-bye to all this? Because you don't have to, honestly. You can change your mind. Even now."

"Shut up and fuck me," Alain whispered. "Oh, my God, this feels so good I think I'm going to—"

"Die?" Ulrich said.

"Come," Alain corrected. "Yes, baby, just like that, do me just like that. Oh, you are so good, such a stud. Now come on and kiss my neck. Right there, baby. Put your lips right there."

Alain suddenly shoved Ulrich's head into his throat with all his might, and Ulrich's reflexes took over. He bit deep, and gasped at the wealth that filled his mouth. Then a smack on his ass reminded him to keep his butt moving.

"Harder," Alain said, and Ulrich didn't know if he meant the bite or the fuck, so he doubled the force of both, and Alain's cum spilled between their bellies as his life ran free and ran out into Ulrich's grieving mouth.

He called the bar before he left Alain's apartment, and left an urgent message for Harvey. Then he carefully rifled the mind of everybody in the building and made sure they had seen and heard nothing, not even fucking. He got on his bike, and he rode away slowly, deliberately lagging until the sun came up and scorched his worthless hide. By the time he got home, he was burned all over, but he had no more tears. He thought he would never cry again.

He fell asleep clicking the ball in his tongue against the left fang, the right fang, the left fang again, a lonely little ditty that could only be played by someone whose mouth was not being glutted by Alain's voracious tongue.

The Mausoleum: Notes on the Contributors

C. Dean Andersson's published novels of dark fantasy and horror number ten, five under the pen name of Asa Drake. They include Andersson's Dallas Horror Trilogy *(Torture Tomb, Raw Pain Max, Fiend)*. He has also written two prequels to Stoker's *Dracula: Crimson Kisses* and *I Am Dracula* (*CK* was an Asa Drake book co-written with Nina Romberg). *I Am Dracula* is being reissued in October 1996 to coincide with the release of the second book in the "I Am" series, *I Am Frankenstein*. The third "I Am" novel, *I Am the Mummy*, is in progress.

Poppy Z. Brite is a native of New Orleans. She has had very little formal training in any field, but has been writing since she was five years old (and telling stories into tape recorders before that). She has published three novels: *Lost Souls, Drawing Blood*, and most recently *Exquisite Corpse*, a tale of serial murder, cannibalistic love, and the politics of victimhood and disease. Her short-story collection, *Wormwood* (also published as *Swamp Foetus*), is available from Dell Books. She is currently at work on a biography of rock diva Courtney Love. Poppy Z. Brite lives in New Orleans with a small menagerie and her husband Christopher, a chef.

Pat Califia is working on a vampire novel called *Mortal Companion*. This story is excerpted from that work. She is also working on a novel, *The Code*, and *Sex Changes*, a book about the formation of transgendered identities and communities. Other books in print include *Melting Point*, a collection of short stories, and *Public Sex*, a collection of essays about sexual politics. She exists only to make others happy.

M. Christian lives in a too-old house in San Francisco and really likes writing about sex and death. His work can be found in *Best Gay Erotica 1996, Best American Erotica 1994, Noirotica, Happily Ever After* and *Grave Passions: Tales of the Gay Supernatural.*

Kevin Killian is a poet, playwright, novelist whose books include *Desiree, Shy, Bedrooms Have Windows, Santa* and *Little Men.* With Lew Ellingham, he is writing a biography of the American poet Jack Spicer (1925-1965). He lives in San Francisco, where for six years he has been working on a new novel, *Spread Eagle.*

Nancy Kilpatrick has published the vampire novels *Child of the Night, Near Death* and *As One Dead* (a collaboration). Under her nom de plume, she has authored five pansexual erotic horror novels and edited four anthologies. Her collections include *Sex and the Single Vampire, Endorphins* and *The Vampire Stories of Nancy Kilpatrick.* She has scripted four stories for the comic Vamperotica and a graphic novel. She's published about one hundred short stories and has twice been both a Bram Stoker Award finalist and an Aurora Award finalist. In 1992, she won the Arthur Ellis Award for best mystery story.

William J. Mann is the author of *Wisecracker: The Life and Times of Billy Haines.* He is the editor of *Grave Passions: Tales from the Gay Supernatural* and has written for numerous publications, including *The Boston Phoenix, Architectural Digest, The Advocate* and *Wilde.* His stories and essays have appeared in *Men on Men 6, Sister & Brother, Queer View Mirror, Happily Ever After, Looking for Mr. Preston, Shadows of Love, Wanderlust* and the forthcoming *Queerly Classed.* The former publisher of the award-winning magazine *Metroline,* he is currently completing a novel.

David Nickle has had stories published in *On Spec, Northern Frights 1, 2,* and *3, Christmas Magic, Tesseracts 4, Transversions, Valkyrie Magazine* and *The Year's Best Fantasy and Horror* eighth annual collection. In 1993, his story "The Toy Mill" (co-written with Karl Schroeder) won the Canadian Aurora Award for best short work in English. He lives in Toronto, where he works as a political reporter for a local community newspaper.

At the age of twelve, **Ron Oliver** was kicked out of Boy Scouts for being "unable to live up to [their] moral code," and subsequently became an award-winning writer and director with numerous films and television episodes to his credit. Although his popular story "Monster Cock," co-written with childhood pal and whipping boy Michael Rowe, appeared in *Flesh and the Word 3*, "Bela Lugosi Is Dead" is Ron's first solo work, not counting a videotape currently circulating on the Internet. Ron lives in West Hollywood, California, usually alone except for occasional visits by his adopted son, Goose.

"Feeding" is **Carol Queen's** first vampire story, but she's had a soft, wet spot for the Undead since at least her first Roman Polanski flick. She is the author of many erotic stories and essays about sex and of *Exhibitionism for the Shy*. With Lawrence Schimel, she co-edited *Switch Hitters: Lesbians Write Gay Male Erotica and Gay Men Write Lesbian Erotica*.

D. Travers Scott's muddy tracks can be found in: *Harper's, Drummer, New Art Examiner, X-X-X Fruit, Steam, Pucker Up, Reclaiming the Heartland, Best Gay Erotica 1996, Ritual Sex, Switch Hitters, Happily Ever After: Erotic Fairy Tales for Men* and numerous 'zines. He edited a recent issue of *P-form* on performance and the pornographic, which is being expanded into an anthology, *Strategic Sex*. He lives in Seattle.

Wickie Stamps, editor of *Drummer* magazine, is a writer whose works appear in *Sister and Brother, Looking for Mr. Preston, Doing It for Daddy, Leatherfolk, Queer View Mirror, Best Lesbian Erotica 1996, Switch Hitters* and *Flashpoint*. Her work is forthcoming in *Close Calls* and *Once Upon a Time: Erotic Fairy Tales for Women*.

Thomas S. Roche is a writer and editor of horror, crime fiction and erotica. His short fiction has appeared in such anthologies as *Razor Kiss, Ritual Sex, Dark Angels, Splatterpunks 2, Best Gay Erotica 1996, Best American Erotica 1996* and *The Mammoth Book of International Erotica,* and is forthcoming in *Gothic Ghosts, Hot Blood 8, Northern Frights 4* and *The Mammoth Book of Pulp Fiction.* He has also written for such magazines as *Black Sheets, Blue Blood, Boudoir Noir, Cupido, Marquis* and *Paramour.* His first anthology, *Noirotica,* is a book of erotic crime-noir stories. His collection *Dark Fiber* will be available from Masquerade Books in 1997.

Michael Rowe is the author of the critically acclaimed *Writing Below the Belt: Conversations with Erotic Authors.* Some of his most recent anthologized essays appear in *Sister and Brother: Lesbians and Gay Men Write About Their Lives Together, Friends and Lovers: Gay Men Write About the Families They Create,* and *Looking for Mr. Preston.* Some of his most recent fiction appears in *Queer View Mirror, Northern Frights 3, Flashpoint,* and *Best Gay Erotica 1996.* His erotic horror fiction (co-authored with Ron Oliver) appears in *Flesh and the Word 3* and *Flesh Fantastic.* He makes his home in Toronto where he is senior writer at *Fab* magazine.

BOOKS FROM CLEIS PRESS

Sexual Politics
Forbidden Passages: Writings Banned in Canada, introductions by Pat Califia and Janine Fuller.
ISBN: 1-57344-019-1 14.95 paper.

Public Sex: The Culture of Radical Sex by Pat Califia.
ISBN: 0-939416-89-1 12.95 paper.

Sex Work: Writings by Women in the Sex Industry, edited by Frédérique Delacoste and Priscilla Alexander.
ISBN: 0-939416-11-5 16.95 paper.

Susie Bright's Sexual Reality: A Virtual Sex World Reader by Susie Bright.
ISBN: 0-939416-59-X 9.95 paper.

Susie Bright's Sexwise by Susie Bright.
ISBN: 1-57344-002-7 10.95 paper.

Susie Sexpert's Lesbian Sex World by Susie Bright.
ISBN: 0-939416-35-2 9.95 paper.

Erotic Literature
Best Gay Erotica 1996, selected by Scott Heim, edited by Michael Ford.
ISBN: 1-57344-052-3 12.95 paper.

Best Lesbian Erotica 1996, selected by Heather Lewis, edited by Tristan Taormino.
ISBN: 1-57344-054-X 12.95 paper.

Serious Pleasure: Lesbian Erotic Stories and Poetry, edited by the Sheba Collective.
ISBN: 0-939416-45-X 9.95 paper.

Switch Hitters: Lesbians Write Gay Male Erotica and Gay Men Write Lesbian Erotica, edited by Carol Queen and Lawrence Schimel.
ISBN: 1-57344-021-3 12.95 paper.

Gender Transgression
Body Alchemy: Transsexual Portraits by Loren Cameron.
ISBN: 1-57344-062-0 24.95 paper.

Dagger: On Butch Women, edited by Roxxie, Lily Burana, Linnea Due.
ISBN: 0-939416-82-4 14.95 paper.

I Am My Own Woman: The Outlaw Life of Charlotte von Mahlsdorf, translated by Jean Hollander.
ISBN: 1-57344-010-8 12.95 paper.

Lesbian and Gay Studies
The Case of the Good-For-Nothing Girlfriend by Mabel Maney.
ISBN: 0-939416-91-3 10.95 paper.

The Case of the Not-So-Nice Nurse by Mabel Maney.
ISBN: 0-939416-76-X 9.95 paper.

Nancy Clue and the Hardly Boys in A Ghost in the Closet by Mabel Maney.
ISBN: 1-57344-012-4 10.95 paper.

Different Daughters: A Book by Mothers of Lesbians, second edition, edited by Louise Rafkin.
ISBN: 1-57344-050-7 12.95 paper.

Different Mothers: Sons & Daughters of Lesbians Talk about Their Lives, edited by Louise Rafkin.
ISBN: 0-939416-41-7 9.95 paper.

A Lesbian Love Advisor by Celeste West.
ISBN: 0-939416-26-3 9.95 paper.

Thrillers & Dystopias
Another Love by Erzsébet Galgóczi.
ISBN: 0-939416-51-4 8.95 paper.

Dirty Weekend: A Novel of Revenge
by Helen Zahavi.
ISBN: 0-939416-85-9 10.95 paper.

Only Lawyers Dancing
by Jan McKemmish.
ISBN: 0-939416-69-7 9.95 paper.

The Wall by Marlen Haushofer.
ISBN: 0-939416-54-9 9.95 paper.

Vampires & Horror
Dark Angels: Lesbian Vampire Stories,
edited by Pam Keesey.
ISBN 1-7344-014-0 10.95 paper.

*Daughters of Darkness: Lesbian
Vampire Stories,* edited by Pam Keesey.
ISBN: 0-939416-78-6 9.95 paper.

*Women Who Run with the Werewolves:
Tales of Blood, Lust and Metamorphosis,*
edited by Pam Keesey.
ISBN: 1-57344-057-4 12.95 paper.

*Sons of Darkness: Tales of Men, Blood
and Immortality,* edited by
Michael Rowe and Thomas S. Roche.
ISBN: 1-57344-059-0 12.95 paper.

Debut Novels
Memory Mambo by Achy Obejas.
ISBN: 1-57344-017-5 12.95 paper.

*We Came All The Way from Cuba So
You Could Dress Like This?: Stories*
by Achy Obejas.
ISBN: 0-939416-93-X 10.95 paper.

Seeing Dell by Carol Guess
ISBN: 1-57344-023-X 12.95 paper.

World Literature
A Forbidden Passion
by Cristina Peri Rossi.
ISBN: 0-939416-68-9 9.95 paper.

*Half a Revolution: Contemporary
Fiction by Russian Women,*
edited by Masha Gessen.
ISBN 1-57344-006-X $12.95 paper.

*The Little School: Tales of
Disappearance and Survival in
Argentina* by Alicia Partnoy.
ISBN: 0-939416-07-7 9.95 paper.

Peggy Deery: An Irish Family at War
by Nell McCafferty.
ISBN: 0-939416-39-5 9.95 paper.

Politics of Health
*The Absence of the Dead Is Their Way
of Appearing*
by Mary Winfrey Trautmann.
ISBN: 0-939416-04-2 8.95 paper.

Don't: A Woman's Word
by Elly Danica.
ISBN: 0-939416-22-0 8.95 paper

*Voices in the Night: Women Speaking
About Incest,* edited by Toni A.H.
McNaron and Yarrow Morgan.
ISBN: 0-939416-02-6 9.95 paper.

*With the Power of Each Breath: A
Disabled Women's Anthology,* edited by
Susan Browne, Debra Connors and
Nanci Stern.
ISBN: 0-939416-06-9 10.95 paper.

Sex Guides

The Good Vibrations Guide to Sex:
How to Have Safe, Fun Sex in the '90s
by Cathy Winks and Anne Semans.
ISBN: 0-939416-84-0 16.95 paper.

Good Sex: Real Stories from Real People,
second edition, by Julia Hutton.
ISBN: 1-57344-000-0 14.95 paper.

Comix

Dyke Strippers: Lesbian Cartoonists A
to Z, edited by Roz Warren.
ISBN: 1-57344-008-6 16.95 paper.

The Night Audrey's Vibrator Spoke: A
Stonewall Riots Collection
by Andrea Natalie.
ISBN: 0-939416-64-6 8.95 paper.

Revenge of Hothead Paisan: Homicidal
Lesbian Terrorist by Diane DiMassa.
ISBN: 1-57344-016-7 16.95 paper.

Travel & Cooking

Betty and Pansy's Severe Queer Review
of San Francisco
by Betty Pearl and Pansy.
ISBN: 1-57344-056-6 10.95 paper.

Food for Life & Other Dish,
edited by Lawrence Schimel.
ISBN: 1-57344-061-2 14.95 paper.

Writer's Reference

Putting Out: The Essential Publishing
Resource Guide For Gay and Lesbian
Writers, third edition,
by Edisol W. Dotson.
ISBN: 0-939416-87-5 12.95 paper.

Women & Honor: Some Notes on Lying
by Adrienne Rich.
ISBN: 0-939416-44-1 3.95 paper.

Since 1980, Cleis Press has published progressive books by women. We welcome your order and will ship your books as quickly as possible. Individual orders must be prepaid (U.S. dollars only). Please add 15% shipping. PA residents add 6% sales tax. Mail orders: Cleis Press, PO Box 8933, Pittsburgh PA 15221. MasterCard and Visa orders: include account number, exp. date, and signature. FAX your credit card order: (412) 937-1567. Or, phone us Mon-Fri, 9 am - 5 pm EST: (412) 937-1555 or (800) 780-2279.